INTO THE
JUNGLE
THE TEAM BOOK II

D1715329

DAVID M. SALKIN

A POST HILL PRESS BOOK

ISBN: 978-1-68261-227-9
ISBN (eBook): 978-1-61868-858-3

Into the Jungle:
The Team Book Two
© 2015 by David M. Salkin
All Rights Reserved

Cover Design by David Walker

Post Hill
PRESS

Post Hill Press

posthillpress.com

Also by David M. Salkin

Hard Carbon
Deep Black Sea
Crescent Fire
Necessary Extremes
The MOP
Forever Hunger
Deep Down

The TEAM

Coach: Chris Mackey, CIA

US Navy Seals:
Chris Cascaes, Chief Petty Officer, SEAL team leader
Al Carlosgio – "Moose"
Vinny "Ripper" Colgan
Ray Jensen
Pete McCoy
Jon Cohen
Ryan O'Conner

Marine Recondos:
Eric Hodges
Earl Jones
Raul Santos

CIA:
Ernesto Perez, "Ernie P."
Joe Smith, "Smitty"
Cory Stewart

Army Rangers:
Lance Woods
Jake Koches

"The Nation that makes a great distinction between its scholars and its warriors will have its thinking done by cowards and its fighting done by fools."

Thucydides, 5th c. BC
Soldier and Statesman

AUTHOR'S NOTE

Thanks for taking a peek inside the cover. I hope you read the story and find yourself immersed so deeply into the jungle that you forget what was bothering you at work, or how many chores you still have left to do. In fact, I hope you stay up so late trying to finish this book that you're tired the next morning. It's a quick read, and I don't think you'll be bored.

The Tri-Border Region of South America is, in fact, a haven for narco-terrorists, Middle Eastern Jihadists, and some very bad people. Because they move around at the border of three countries, they're "no one's problem." Actually, they're everyone's problem. For Americans who think border security is just some political football, please wake up and smell the cocaine. I mean roses. Every day, people enter this nation illegally. And not all of them are the hard working folks that take agricultural jobs. If tens of thousands of children can simply walk across the border, how many terrorists, gang bangers and drug smugglers do you think can get in every year? Do some reading about the tri-border region. If this book doesn't keep you up late at night, the facts should.

The Team II is the continuation of the adventures of a special group of war fighters and CIA operatives that began in the Middle East in book one. There was actually a *real* team that was formed in Southeast Asia in the late sixties as the Navy All-Star Baseball Team. Except there was no such team—it was just an excellent cover story for secret missions. While this book is complete fabrication, the concept of the team was taken from those real missions, and those real warriors. This book is dedicated to Al (Moose) and his "teammates", who risked life and limb for their country.

At this moment, all over the world, American men and women are at risk to protect this great nation. They wear all types of uniforms, or no uniform at all. There's too many to list, but if you're reading this and you know it means you—thank you.

Every book I write is dedicated to the same groups of people. My family, my friends, my readers, and the brave men and women who have served, are serving, or will one day serve this Great Nation. "Freedom isn't free" isn't some corny t-shirt slogan. I know too many people who have been directly impacted by war and terrorist attacks not to fully understand that we are so very blessed to live in these United States of America.

Lastly, there is a real Chris Cascaes. Even after a forty year friendship, he is forced to fight for the life of his character in each book. Chris...I hope you make it. I can't guarantee you anything, though...

CHAPTER 1

Dex Murphy and Chris Mackey walked the long hallway to Darren Davis's office. There were people in the halls, all walking briskly with plenty of stress in their faces. It was clearly a busy place. Davis was sixty-two, but starting to look older. He had been asked directly by Wallace Holstrum, the Director of CIA, not to retire even though he had been eligible for a few years. His department was one of the busiest in the building, and Darren was good at what he did. He managed dozens of agents personally, as well as his managers, who had their own field agents. He understood politics, both here and abroad, and he knew the Middle East map as well as the United States. While his days in the field had ended in Saigon, he was sharp as ever, and had been a big reason that terrorists were unsuccessful since 9-11 in hitting the US again.

Darrin was scribbling on a yellow pad, his usual pose, when they walked into his office. He saw Chris Mackey and stood up, then walked around his desk and gave him a hug, something pretty rare for Davis.

"Welcome home, Chris," he smiled. "It's been too long."

"Thanks, Darren. Two weeks on the beach and I felt human again. I was sure I was done after 'Wrecking Ball', but then I saw those guys play ball and my head started working again. Actually got excited about working again…"

Darren laughed and sat on his desk. "Chris, guys like you belong in the field. It doesn't matter how old you are, you'd never be happy sitting at a desk here or working security at a mall. Besides, we need you."

Chris and Dex sat down in two black leather chairs facing the boss, who walked around and sat back in his own chair.

Darren looked at the two of them and said, "I don't even know where to begin. There is so much activity right now there must be a hundred jobs that need doing. Problem is, we need to find the right kind of atmosphere to make it work with your baseball team."

Dex added, "Yeah, we had talked about this earlier as well. I get nervous sending an entire team of agents overtly out into the world. If their cover gets blown, we'd lose more agents in one day than we have in a decade."

"Which is precisely why we have to make sure it doesn't," said Darren. "I am hesitant about sending you back to the Middle East too soon. I've been in constant contact with my counterpart in our Latin American Department. Intelligence from my agents in the Middle East, including the same source that gave us that truck full of cash, have told us that Al Qaeda is funding and working with a few groups in Mexico and Latin America. We all know how porous the border is between Mexico and the US. Makes sense that they'd try to get through there. Mexican cops are a lot easier to buy than the Royal Canadian Mounted Police. We've been discussing a 'Latin American tour' for your team. Still lots to work out, but that may be your next assignment. Just thought you'd want to know ahead of time."

Mackey folded his arms across his chest. "Same type of assignments? Intercepting money and weapons, that sort of thing?"

"Not necessarily, Chris," said Darren. Chris understood.

"Well, a few of my guys speak fluent Spanish. Guess that will help."

Davis continued, "Hezbollah and Al Qaeda have both been working in the tri-border area of Brazil, Paraguay and Argentina. They are well funded from coke money as well as counterfeiting, and have plenty of support from local radical factions. There is no shortage of rebels and terrorists out there. They are well organized and heavily armed. Every drug lord has his own little army, and anything that happens from drugs in the US, to counterfeit bills in the US, to violence against the local governments—it's all considered a victory for these people. We're trying to acquire significant targets to break up their organizations, and your team might be the way to go. One or two agents can't get in there. We have a lot to plan and discuss in the next few weeks. We'll talk again soon after I meet with the director and the Latin desk chief.

Davis stood up, signaling that the meeting was over. "Look Chris, there's nothing concrete yet. Hell, you could end up in Sierra Leone for all I know, but for now, assume you're heading south of the border unless I tell you otherwise. We're gathering intel, following some leads, that sort of stuff. We have a few agents on the ground nearby, but they are intelligence gatherers only."

Chris felt a pang of shame. In other words, they weren't "killers" like him. He stood up. "Okay, Darren. We'll keep the guys working and wait to see what pans out. Good to see you."

They shook hands. Dex smiled and said, "It's good to see you, too, Mack. You did a helluva' job in Qatar." Mackey and Dex left Darren's office and headed out to find their team, busy training on the latest gizmos and intelligence gathering devices down in the sub-basement.

CHAPTER 2

Jungles near Ciudad del Este, Paraguay

Enrique Antonio Vega was smoking a fat cigar and drinking a moderately cold beer while he watched the bricks of cocaine being carefully packed into the bags for the natives that would carry the drugs over the Brazilian border. Vega's operation averaged twenty million dollars a month in drug money, supplying big dealers all over South and Central America, who, in turn, supplied US drug dealers. The average Joe in the US snorting the coke up his nose didn't bother to learn that the money he spent ultimately went to people who were trying to kill him.

Enrique puffed his cigar and watched the last bag packed and tied to long poles as his small army stood around with their AK-47s at the ready. They were really just there for show. Here in the deep jungle, no one would dare come anywhere near his operation, and if they did, he would know hours ahead of time. The Guarani natives in this part of the jungle still lived like they had for a few thousand years, except now they would transport huge quantities of drugs through jungle trails for Enrique Vega in exchange for the most modest of items. Their payment for walking miles through almost impassable jungle carrying hundreds of pounds of cocaine was blankets, steel cook pots, mirrors, knives, and rainproof slicks to use as improved roofing materials for their "ogas", the long rectangular houses where they lived. Each oga was almost fifty meters long and housed more than fifty nuclear families. There

4

were five ogas in their little jungle clearing, under one central chief. That chief, the "abrubicha," was the head of the village and held absolute authority over his people. Vega had made a deal with him three years earlier to protect his people from any government encroachment, and gave him regular gifts of steel knives and beaded jewelry from the city of Ciudad del Este to make him look more important.

For his part, the abrubicha, called Kuka by his people, made sure the packages were delivered each week along the almost invisible trails that stretched from Paraguay into Brazil near the Parana River. The Guarani people had once been nomads, moving their villages whenever the abrubicha saw fit. When Brazil and Paraguay became "civilized," the Portuguese enslaved or killed most of the Guarani. Jesuit Missionaries managed to save some of them from the slave traders, but eventually the missions failed and closed, and the Guarani were either butchered or forced deeper into the jungle. This tribe of "Pampidos Guarani" were the direct descendants of peoples that had lived near this very spot since the twelve-hundreds A.D.. Kuka's ancestors had all been kings of their people. Kuka was the first drug smuggler, however.

The fact that it was cocaine was fairly lost on Kuka and his people. He and his people had been chewing coca leaves forever. Typically before battles against other tribes or Portuguese slavers, his warriors would get high as a kite on coca leaves. Those they killed in battle were typically eaten afterwards as a way of honoring fellow warriors. The word Guarani translated to warrior, and these were fierce people. They fought only with bows and arrows and macanas, wooden sword-like weapons. And while they had seen the AK-47s of Vega's men, and understood the power they possessed and protection they offered from others who might come, they had no interest in using them. They were warriors that preferred to be up close and personal when it was time to fight. If they were not soaked with the blood of their enemies, they did not feel as though they had sufficiently proven their bravery.

Enrique finished his cigar and walked over to Kuka. Vega had learned enough of their language over the past three years to be able to communicate with the chief. He instructed him to go east into the morning sun, up the river trail where he would be met by boats. It was one of only three routes they ever used. Vega's Brazilian contacts would load the coke into their high-speed boat and move up the Parana River all the way to the falls. Once there, they would unload the cargo on to waiting trucks that would follow dirt roads to an airstrip where the coke would be flown all over the Western hemisphere.

Eight pairs of Pampidos natives walked with long wooden poles between them over their shoulders. Hundred pound sacks of cocaine were tied to the poles between them, and in this manner, these stalwart people could walk for days without complaining or showing fatigue. It was the same method they had used for generations to carry their houses, game they had killed, or captured enemies. The trip to the river typically took two days, although once, when Vega was rushed, they had made it in one. They walked through the night without stopping that trip, something that the Pampidos didn't like to do. The Guarani believed that dangerous animal souls stalked the jungle at night, and it took Kuka himself going on that trip to guarantee the arrival of the shipment on time. He also had to take thirty of his most ferocious warriors to protect the skittish porters.

For this trip, the sixteen porters would travel with only eight warriors to protect them, as well as two other pairs of porters who carried the pieces they would use to make a quick shelter in the jungle for their overnight stay. It was always important to them to be "inside" at night, even it only meant surrounding themselves with a few pieces of wood and a tarp overhead. The animal gods would never venture inside the homes.

Enrique patted the chief's strong shoulder. He told him the boat would meet them by midday sun tomorrow. Kuka gave instructions to his people, who then took off silently through the jungle. It always amazed Enrique how quiet they were. Even his best men made *some* noise shuffling through the thick leaves of the jungle. But not these people—these people moved silently, like ghosts drifting invisibly through the shadows of the jungle. He smiled as they disappeared in a matter of seconds. Vega turned and headed back to his small wooden house, built by Kuka's people just for him. He had kept his Hezbollah friends waiting too long, and didn't want them grumpy when they discussed weapon prices.

CHAPTER 3

CIA Training Facility

It had been an intense four weeks, but one that the team had enjoyed immensely. When they had time out of the classroom, they would head over to nearby colleges and play baseball against the college teams to keep improving and try and resemble a real baseball team. Their classroom time was spent trying out new gear and weapons. They used everything from miniature infrared sensors to monitor enemy movements to satellite uplink phones and computers for everything from navigating to communicating to spying on positions from deep space using laptops. The technology was amazing, and although some of what they saw they had used in the past, they had never seen such lightweight, miniature versions. Evidently, it was okay for soldiers to hump eighty-five pounds of gear, but CIA agents preferred something about two ounces that fit in a pocket.

They worked out as hard as ever, although the SEALs complained about the lack of swimming. They pushed their bodies and minds as far as they could, and then a little more. By the end of the fourth week, even the rangers and marines were chanting, *"The only easy day was yesterday,"* something they inherited from the SEALs. They would run, not jog, a minimum of five miles a day, some days farther, and for the first time since they'd been together actually had some inter-service rivalry. Vinny "Ripper" Colgan ended up winning the pushup contest. They didn't even *have* the contest until they had finished their workout. By then, they were all totally whipped, but the SEALs insisted that you didn't *start* counting your reps until they already hurt. The marines laughed and gave the standard line about "pain is weakness leaving the body" and then they all got down and went pushup for pushup. After seventy-five pushups, the group slowly began dropping out, one by one.

In the end, it was Raul Santos, proudly representing the USMC, and Ripper Colgan getting the encouragement of the SEALs. By the time they hit one hundred, the pushups were taking four seconds each. Their arms were shaking and the sweat dripped off their chins as they faced each other only two feet apart. By one hundred and fifteen, they were both screaming at the top of their lungs with each push off the floor, delighting the rest of the inspired bunch. On pushup one hundred twenty-two, Raul dropped on his face, completely physically exhausted. Ripper finished his and flopped, then rolled on his back as the SEALs pulled him to his feet cheering wildly. They were good-natured about the win, and joined Earl Jones and Eric Hodges in helping Santos off the floor, too.

Ripper gave Raul a hug, and the two of them just stood there, like two heavyweights at the end of a championship fight, leaning on each other and trying to breathe. Neither one could lift his arms.

"You're a tough lil' Sonofabitch," said Ripper quietly.

"You, too," grumbled Raul. It was all he could muster

After the workout and pushups were finished, the team showered and changed into black jumpsuits for night operations. They ate dinner and then attended a briefing on "stalking and destroying a target at night with no ambient light, using night vision goggles and GIS directional tracking equipment." The workshop lasted three hours. When it was over, it was almost midnight, and they loaded buses and traveled dirt roads deep into the CIA owned property where they would be unceremoniously dropped off in the middle of nowhere.

They were given two map waypoints to find, each waypoint location having a small box sitting on the forest floor full of tasks to complete. The first box contained the location of the second waypoint. After the second waypoint, they were required to set infrared sensors and setup an ambush against unknown enemies who would be trying to sneak up on them. It was similar to courses they had all gone through in Special Forces training, but the equipment was smaller, lighter and better. They were given three hours to complete their task, which covered an area of approximately two square miles of thick forest. It was a new moon, and without goggles on, they couldn't see their hands in front of their faces.

Mackey was a smart guy, but even he was amazed at how good Cascaes was in the field. He and his SEAL team had obviously been through plenty together, and they operated quickly and silently. Cascaes had come up with the idea of splitting their team in two, so one could find the first waypoint while the other stayed fresh and moved slower covering their rear. As soon as the first group got the coordinates of the second spot, the second team would become lead, moving faster on fresh legs to the assigned place. Using this technique, they arrived at waypoint two almost forty-five minutes faster than the CIA trainers had anticipated. They quickly set up the sensors in a very wide perimeter and set up multiple ambush points, then guided the first team into a second ambush area.

Once the sensors were in the ground, it was just a matter of hunkering down and waiting. The small sensors picked up the tiniest vibrations, and showed the location of the movement on the tiny computer that Cascaes was watching from his position in the roots of a huge Oak. The "red team" of CIA agents that were assigned to ambush them arrived quietly, but couldn't fool the sensors. Cascaes quickly directed his men into ambush positions and they were able to "take out" all six of the red team trainers in record time with complete silence.

Once the "bad guys" were "killed," the mission wasn't over. They were then given twenty minutes to get back to their bus, or have to walk back to their rooms almost eight miles away. They were having none of that. Cascaes quickly navigated their course to the bus, and knowing they had gotten all of the bad guys out of the way, they sprinted through the forest all the way back to the bus. Being used to carrying combat packs that often weighed over one hundred pounds with weapons and ammo, running an operation with only the lightest of gear was a breeze. They were standing at the bus with six minutes to spare, a course record. Mackey was the only one really winded, and he vomited as soon as they stopped running. The team knew better than to bust his chops. The guy was getting older, but he had proven himself a warrior enough times to be beyond harassment. Jones quietly gave him his canteen to wash his mouth out, and the silent nod was a humble thank you.

CHAPTER 4

Jungles near Ciudad del Este, Paraguay

Enrique Vega walked into the small cabin to find three men drinking hot tea on the woven mat that was the floor.

"Don't get up," he said as he entered.

Their accents were thick, and they spoke English since they didn't speak any Spanish. Vega spoke English fluently, better than the Arabs in fact, so they were able to communicate without a problem.

"How was your trip?" he asked as he sat.

"*Long*. I am not used to the humidity. It saps your strength. I have been here a dozen times, and every time it is the same thing. Mosquitoes, diarrhea, and this damned humidity. I don't know how you live out here in this Hell," said Raman Qasim, the local contact for Hezbollah in the tri-border region between Brazil, Argentina and Paraguay.

Ali Aziz, an Al Qaeda operative and huge weapons smuggler, spoke in a quieter voice. He was an older man, perhaps sixty, with his beard now almost fully gray. "The shipments you requested are getting more expensive to transport here. Shipping is tracked closer in the ports. The roads to the interior are terrible. And the local police are getting more expensive each trip."

Enrique nodded. "Yes, the police are becoming quite a thorn. The Americans have been in the city. Every time they come, they stir up a hornet's nest. Then they go, and it costs me twice as much to get the same things done. But you were able to bring the C4 and RPGs?"

Ali smiled. "Of course, my brother. But we have a favor to ask—to be 'negotiated,' rather."

"Oh?" asked Enrique. He was not one for surprises.

"A few years ago, you were able to carry out an operation for us against the Israeli Embassy in Argentina. It was most successful," said Ali.

"Yes, and it also had this entire area crawling with commandos from all over the world for six months. It was most inconvenient. We were forced to move another ten kilometers deeper into this Godforsaken jungle and we lost weeks of production."

"But you rebuilt, and now your operation is even larger," said Ali, smiling. "You have quite a little army of workers here, don't you?" he asked, referring to the large Guarani tribe.

"True. We're so deep in the jungle now that we don't have much to worry about. The planes don't patrol here, and even if they did, the canopy is too thick for them to be able to see anything. If anyone tried to find us on foot, my Guaranis would know immediately and alert me. I have more than enough men and firepower here, thanks to you."

"Yes, back to the firepower. It has been a very good partnership, yes? Your cash has helped us to support our brothers who fight the government that interferes with your business, and the weapons we provide to you allow you to take care of your own priorities." Ali stroked his gray beard and smiled.

Hakim Bin-Salaam, a fit young Arab in jungle fatigues and a green beret, spoke up for the first time. "Our weapons have also helped you 'corner the market,' so to speak, no? The Ortiz organization, the Montoya family, the Cortez Cartel…they have all simply disappeared, yes? If the rumors are true, some of them were even cannibalized. Now who could have done such a thing?"

"The tri-border area is a dangerous place, no doubt," said Enrique with an evil smile slowly spreading across his face. "So what is this favor?"

Ali pulled a leather folder from inside his blouse. He unzipped it and removed photographs of people and buildings. Ali carefully laid all of the photos flat on the mat facing Enrique. He pointed to a man in a suit and tie in the first picture.

"That is the American Ambassador to Paraguay, James McKnight. He and his staff will be in the city for a conference on 'The Americas Trading Partnership.' We would very much like to see his motorcade destroyed in a most visible, violent and terrifying fashion. Television crews will be filming their arrival in front of the Paraguayan Center for International Trade. The entire world could get an opportunity to see that Al Qaeda is alive and well in the western hemisphere." Ali sat back, twirling his beard around his fingers.

"A media event," said Enrique quietly. He frowned. "Killing an American will start a war here, Ali. They will fill the jungle with soldiers again. I don't want to have to start up all over again somewhere else. The trip to Brazil is already two days."

Hakim clucked his tongue. "No, Señor Vega. The attack will clearly be the work of Al Qaeda, not local factions. In fact, our brothers in Iraq will take full credit for the attack. The Americans and local police will not bother you."

Enrique scanned the eyes of the three men in front of him. It was an alliance of convenience only. Vega didn't really care about killing Americans, his best customers in the drug trade. He was more concerned with killing local authorities and government meddlers, as well as his competition. After what the Guaranis had done to the Cortez Cartel, no one would dare start up a competitive cocaine business within a thousand miles. Even Enrique had been slightly horrified when his warriors ate his competition. The skulls still stood on wooden stakes around the village. He lit another cigar and sat back against the wall.

"And you will supply the logistics and weapons, I simply have my men carry out the attack?" asked Enrique quietly. He was very concerned about starting up with the Americans. Their president had proved to be quite willing to use American troops whenever and wherever he felt like it.

"The information is all in that packet," said Ali.

Raman leaned forward, his eyes twinkling with hate. He was the only one that Enrique ever worried about. "We will give you more than enough explosives and detonators to do the job. What is left over is yours. But understand, I want an explosion that will be felt in Washington. The entire staff—McKnight and all of his people. And anyone else that would sit down with that crusader dog. *Hundreds* of casualties, Señor Vega, not dozens." The venom of his hate made his voice come out like a serpent's hiss. Enrique's skin crawled. Not because he abhorred violence—quite the contrary, he killed everyone that stood in his way—but this man Raman, he was *scary* crazy.

Enrique sat for a moment looking at the photos, buying a few seconds to think about his options. There were very few. He needed their weapons to maintain his private army. He hesitated only because he clearly understood what Raman wanted—a total massacre.

"When exactly will this take place?" asked Enrique.

"The first of June. You have several weeks to make your plans. We have supplied the maps, their travel plans, and the personnel that will be attending the event—everything you need. We want maximum damage. There will be enough explosives to take out a city block. And that is precisely what we would like you to do."

CHAPTER 5

CIA HQ

Darren Davis was at a high-level meeting with CIA Director Wallace Holstrum and the Chief of the Latin Desk, Leah Pereira. She was to Central and South America what Darren Davis was to the Middle East. Leah was forty-four years old, and one of the youngest women to ever hold such a high-level office inside the Agency. She had grown up in Brazil, the daughter of an American diplomat, and spoke English, Spanish, and Portuguese all equally well. By the age of thirty-one, she had been a CIA secret agent posing as the Assistant Director of the Latin American Employment and Economic Development Office in Panama. After three years there, she returned to the States to work "inside," and had been there ever since, steadily proving herself as an intelligent and capable woman as she worked her way up the chain of command.

She sat across from Darren in her navy blue suit with her chestnut hair pulled in a bun. Her mother had been Brazilian, her father American, and she was a very attractive woman. Darren was used to sitting across from men at most meetings, and considered her a pleasant change. If you had to work, you might as well have something to look at.

Director Holstrum began the meeting. After quick pleasantries, he pulled up a map showing the tri-border region.

"The reason I asked you both to meet with me again about the tri-border region is because of overlapping intelligence coming out of your respective offices. Al Qaeda, Hezbollah,

16

and Hamas are working in this area side by side with the local drug lords. They make quite a cozy little team. Just about everything illegal, insidious, and evil that can be done by a human being is being perpetrated by these people with absolute impunity. Their pockets are deep, and their influence in the region has no bounds. Our people in the field find more people 'on the take' down there than off of it. We can trust no one."

The director pressed a button and changed slides, showing pictures of a dozen Arab looking men. "These are only a handful of the men working in the area. They fly in and out of Venezuela, Argentina and Paraguay like they own the place. Those governments, while cooperating to some degree, with the exception of Venezuela, claim they don't have 'just cause' to pick them up. This is *after* we handed them dozens of case files on these dirt-bags proving their drug connections and weapons smuggling. I'm not sure who's paying whom, but it's the Wild West down there."

The director changed slides again. It was a grainy black and white photo of Enrique Antonio Vega. As soon as his face appeared, Leah quietly said his name.

"That's right, Leah. Our old friend Vega." He looked at Davis, who was unfamiliar with the man. "Enrique Antonio Vega is the single largest cocaine producer and supplier in the tri-border region. Because he is so deep in the jungle, Brazil, Paraguay, and Argentine all point the finger at each other as to whom is supposed to do something about him. In the meantime, he pays officials from all three countries to make sure that they leave him alone. The few officials that did try and do something in Brazil have all ended up dead. The same for his competitors."

He changed slides and showed a Guarani Native. The man was standing in a loincloth only, his black hair in a neat bowl cut around his head. He had a piercing through his lower lip and a few long green feathers tied in the back of his head.

Tattoos on both arms added to his fierce appearance as he stood holding a wooden club and blow-gun.

Davis sat back, surprised at the slide, and looked back at the director waiting for an explanation.

"This is a Guarani Native. They are descendants of the original people of South America. The Portuguese and Spaniards did to them what we did to our own Native Americans. Maybe worse."

Leah interrupted. "Worse. We only killed ours. The Portuguese took hundreds of thousands as slaves and wiped out another couple of million with the Spanish.

"They are still there, however, Darren. A few hundred years later, these people still live in the jungle like our little friend here. With their land disappearing, they have few good choices available, and now it would appear that Señor Vega has a small army of not only his regular goons, but now a couple of hundred Guaranis. Add weapons from Al Qaeda, Hamas, and Hezbollah to the mix, and you have quite an interesting part of the world, don't you?"

"Jesus," was all he could come up with.

Leah spoke up. "Vega has used his Guaranis to wipe out every other drug lord in the area. Many Guaranis live as farmers and cheap laborers on the borders of the jungles, but not his tribe. He has a group of Pampidos Guaranis living and working with him that has reverted to their ancient ways. While the women and children are used to process cocaine side by side with poor people from the Paraguayan countryside, the Guarani men have gone back to hunting, killing and even cannibalism. Vega has pretty much started his own little country out there. One with a GDP that rivals some real countries."

"Why the connection to Middle Eastern Terrorists? They don't usually meddle with drugs," asked Darren.

"Convenience. Vega gets weapons and supplies to run his operation and control the entire area. The terrorists groups get to undermine local governments, kill law enforcement personnel from all over the area, keep the flow of drugs heading to the US, ensure continued violence in the region and force us to spread our resources even thinner," said Director Holstrum.

Darren looked at Leah. "And we've been operating there?"

"Not much," she said with a frown. We have one asset currently working in Paraguay who is very familiar with the area and knows how Vega operates."

"But he can't get close enough to take him out?" asked Davis.

"He's a *she*, actually," she said flashing a fake grin. "And no, she isn't a commando, which is what you would need to get anywhere close to that man. She works for a local charity that helps the Guarani Natives who live on the fringes of society down there."

Director Holstrum said, "Leah is correct, of course. It would take commandos to get anywhere near Vega. The problem is none of those countries will send troops, and they won't allow us to operate inside their borders. Our ambassador to Paraguay, Jim McKnight, is addressing The Americas Trading Partnership next week. He also has a second meeting scheduled with the Paraguayan Vice President to talk about joint US-Paraguayan efforts to go after Vega. If he is successful in convincing Vice President Ortega, the FBI would work with Homeland Security and head south."

"So if it's the Bureau's gig, why are we talking about it?" asked Darren.

"Like I said, *if* the Vice President goes along with his pitch. Frankly, I don't trust Ortega any more than the rest of them down there. If Jim can't get them to play ball, the president may request other options." He folded his arms and looked at the two of them.

"My people down there can supply operational intelligence that would be fairly current, but not much else. I don't have active teams in place there for wet work," said Leah.

"That's where Darren comes in. He may be asked to use a new team for this operation. We won't get ahead of ourselves, though. We'll wait and see how McKnight makes out first. If the 'Fibbies' take the job, then we drop it and go on to something else. But if the Feds don't end up getting a green light, I want you two working together to come up with an alternative for the president. Schedule a meeting with me for next week when you have something to show me. And whatever it is, it will have to be invisible both in and outbound."

CHAPTER 6

CIA Training Facility

The team had taken a break for lunch and the men were enjoying a little downtime when Dex Murphy arrived, unannounced. As soldiers, they stiffened and waited for an "attention on deck," but none came so they continued eating. Mackey and Cascaes, who had been sitting together, both got up.

"To what do we owe the pleasure, Mr. Murphy?" asked Mackey.

"Let's take a walk," he said. "You too, Chris."

They left the small dining hall and walked to a small conference room where they found seats.

"So how's it going? The training I mean," asked Dex.

"I'd say very well. The physical part is too easy, and I've been pushing the guys to do more, but the new toys have been interesting, to say the least," said Mackey.

Dex smiled. "I heard your team set a course record. Training Director Perretti was a little pissed when your guys took out his team in record time. You even made it back to the bus on time. *Nobody* gets back to the bus on time." He was grinning broadly.

Mackey pointed to Cascaes. "We have an excellent navigator."

"Good. You may need one," said Dex, now serious.

The two Chrises looked at each other then back at Dex. "Do we have a mission, sir?" asked Cascaes.

21

"Not yet, but you will begin preparing tomorrow for a possibility. Davis came in my office last night after a meeting with the director and Leah Pereira, the Latin American Desk Chief. I'm sure I don't have to remind you that this conversation is classified." He was looking at Cascaes when he said it, having known Mackey for over twenty years.

"Sir, I am at CIA, and I assume everything is classified Top Secret."

"Good assumption. Now, the American Ambassador to Paraguay, Jim McKnight is heading over for a Summit next week with economic leaders from the region. He also has a private meeting with the Paraguayan Vice President, Hernando Ortega, to try and arrange for an FBI-Homeland Security Taskforce to work with local forces. Seems there is a drug lord down in the jungle, armed by Al Qaeda and other Middle Eastern terror groups that is running his own army down there. We aren't sure that McKnight will be able to convince the vice-president to cooperate."

"What's the matter, we don't pay as well?" asked Mackey, more than a bit cynically.

"Could be. I trust very few people south of our own border. In any case, you are currently the 'Plan B'. Starting tomorrow, you will shift gears and begin preparing for jungle warfare. Your team will be flying down to Florida to go play in the swamps for a few days."

Cascaes actually smiled.

Dex was surprised by his reaction, and Chris could see it in his face.

"No offense, sir, the training here has been beneficial and I've learned some new tricks. But we are fish out of water, sir. My men can't go a month sleeping on clean sheets and eating three meals a day. They'll get soft. A week in the jungle is just what the doctor ordered."

Mackey shook his head. "Yeah, his guys will love it, and I'll probably have a heart attack."

Dex frowned. "So anyway, now you know. There will be a full mission briefing tonight at twenty hundred down in the main conference center where you came in the first day. Have your men packed and ready to go. As soon as the briefing is over, you are heading out. That's all, gentlemen."

They all shook hands and started to head out, but Dex took Mackey by the arm and told him to stay a moment. After Cascaes left, he sat on the desk and faced Mackey.

"Chris, what you said a minute ago, about having a heart attack—Darren and I discussed that as well. If you end up flying in as a baseball team, you'll go as the coach, of course. But we're not sure you should be going on the actual mission. The last time you fought in the jungle, Jimi Hendrix was playing Woodstock."

"Thanks for your concern, Dex, but I'm fine. I ran the course, same as everyone else. If my team is going into the jungle together, I'm going with them." He turned and headed towards the door, then looked back at Dex. "You tell Darren I said thanks, but this old man still knows his way around a jungle. And somebody has to keep an eye on these kids."

CHAPTER 7

Jungles near Ciudad del Este, Paraguay

The Arabs left the camp after the weapons arrived and were paid in full. As promised, they had been most generous in their weapons shipment this time. Besides twenty-four more AK-47s and eight thousand rounds of ammunition, they had also included several blocks of C-4 with remote detonators and three shoulder-fired anti-armor missiles.

Raman and Ali had gone over the travel routes and targets several times with Enrique and three of his best men. The Guaranis would lead a small team of his men through the jungle back to Ciudad del Este to help carry the weapons. Once there, Enrique's regular security force would set up the ambush near the designated building and wait for the convoys to arrive. They would give the Arabs the "show" they wanted and get back into the jungle as fast as possible, where the Guaranis would be waiting to guide them quickly back to their camp.

Enrique smoked a cigar and sat in his hut looking at the timers. He looked at Carlos, his second in command and asked, "You sure you know how to use this stuff?"

"No problem, boss. These remote triggers give us more range than last time. We can place the charges the night before and be half a kilometer away when we set them off. I'll set them off myself, and Felipe will be set up across the square with the rockets. Your friends want a big mess; we'll give them one. Once the explosions go off, it shouldn't be hard to get away. There will be people running everywhere. You want us to hose the crowd too, or just the convoy?"

Enrique rubbed his scruffy chin and thought a moment. "Don't stay too long, but maximum damage."

Carlos grunted. "You have any more of that rum?"

"Yeah, help yourself, but keep it away from the Guaranis. They get too crazy when they're drunk. And make sure your men don't get sloppy. You leave tomorrow morning."

Carlos happily helped himself to one of the bottles of rum that Enrique kept in a small footlocker by his cot. He offered a swig to Enrique, who threw back a shot of the golden liquid, followed by another puff of his cigar.

"Don't get killed, Carlos, I need you here. And make sure no one follows you back here either."

Carlos grunted again and left with the bottle to go find his men. They would drink and clean weapons, and prepare to kill a few hundred people who thought it was going to be just another day.

Enrique followed him out and headed in the opposite direction, down a small path to a large wooden longhouse, similar to the ogas used by the Guaranis as houses. Two of his men sat lazily outside with AK-47s across their laps. They nodded when their boss approached and he ignored them and walked inside.

Long tables and benches stretched from one end of the dirt floor longhouse to the other, and women sat facing each other stacking the dried leaves into bundles that would eventually become hundred pound sacks. Men would come and go from the same door that Enrique had entered through—the only one in the building. They carried large woven bags of the whole dried leaves from a large pit, where they were dried in the sun for two or three days. Once dried, they were brought inside and the women would separate the leaves from the twigs and other botanicals, and then chop them up to uniform size to be wrapped in small square bundles that would then be put together en mass until they had accumulated a hundred pound sack.

Enrique didn't process the cocaine any further than that. He wasn't a chemist, merely a provider of the raw materials. While there would have been much more money in refined cocaine, it would have also required a much more sophisticated operation. He left that to the Columbians and Americans. He was very happy making huge amounts of money while exacting very little effort or risk. The fact that he would have to hit an American target, which would be the riskiest thing he'd ever done, left him very uneasy. Of course, he wouldn't be there himself, but still, he'd hate to lose his men or worse yet, have his men followed back to his operation. He had impressed the chief as best he could, in his very poor Guarani vocabulary, that they needed to be invisible and leave no tracks. Kuka seemed to understand and gave quite a speech to his warriors as they prepared for their trip to "The City of the East", Ciudad del Este.

Enrique walked around the group slowly, watching the women, who wore only small loin clothes. He was eyeing one of the younger ones, perhaps sixteen or so, whose breasts were still standing up perfectly. She caught his stare and immediately began chopping leaves even faster. He approached the older one, the one he called Nanni, and handed her a strand of white plastic beads worth less then a decent pencil. She smiled, showing the gaps in her worn white teeth. He pointed to the young girl. Nanni smiled and spoke rapidly to the girl, who looked somewhat terrified.

While the Guarani women were generally off limits to his men, Enrique took whatever and whoever he wanted in this part of the world. Kuka and he had 'worked it out' a few years earlier with large amounts of gifts to the chief. There were maybe ten women in the village that were off limits—Kuka's two wives and one daughter, and his nieces. Enrique could live with that. He took the young girl by the wrist and led her out of the longhouse. Some of the older women looked concerned, but no one spoke a word. The girl said nothing, although she was scared of what she knew must be coming. The two guards laughed as their boss led her out, walking so quickly she almost had to run to keep up. They commented to each other loud enough to draw a, "Shut up!" from their boss who never broke stride.

Enrique brought her back to his hut, where the girl sat on the floor, backed into a corner. Vega drank some more rum and forced her to drink some. She coughed and her eyes quickly glazed as she drank alcohol for the first time. It had the desired effect of loosening her up, and as soon as she looked calmer, he undressed and unceremoniously raped her. Guarani women were not taught that they had much say in life, so the young girl closed her eyes and tried not to cry as Enrique thrust into his young virgin. He grunted and tried to kiss the unfortunate girl, who squirmed and cried, trying desperately to keep her mouth away from his scruffy face. Guarani men had no facial hair, and she found him physically revolting. His rum and cigar breath nauseated her as he pounded away at her, kissing and biting her smooth skin. She finally began screaming and fighting as he grew rougher, yelling words in Guarani he didn't understand, but was sure meant that she loved every minute of it. He finished a moment later and rolled off of her. She scrambled out of the hut, running into the jungle in tears. Vega slept for almost an hour.

CHAPTER 8

The Glades

The team flew by private jet from Langley to a small deserted airstrip in the Florida Everglades. They were in the Mangrove swamps just north of a small tributary that led into the Broad River. The Broad River flowed west, out towards the Gulf of Mexico, but not before it meandered through some of the toughest swampland a human could have to navigate through. The Alligators along the river were almost as numerous as the snakes, mosquitoes and flies, and humidity of ninety-percent was not uncommon. Moss hanging from the trees gave the area around the airstrip the eerie feeling of a haunted forest out of some B Horror movie.

Dex had given Mackey and Cascaes a fictional mission along the river to practice for the Parana River in Paraguay. Although the flora and fauna was different, the misery of the climate and difficulty of navigation was the same. It wasn't that the team needed practice doing what they had done a thousand times; rather it was that they were given new equipment and needed experience using it. Their new bag of tricks was amazingly lightweight. For soldiers in the field, the weight of their packs was always a problem. It had been that way for hundreds of years. But the CIA had deeper pockets "per soldier" than the armed forces did. Their night vision equipment wasn't much bigger than a pair of sunglasses and would neatly fit in a breast pocket. It was much more convenient than the standard issue for the armed forces, but at twenty times the cost, a regular grunt wouldn't be seeing one for a while. Their new computer equipment was all miniaturized with satellite uplink and communication capabilities better than they had ever used prior. The hardware was waterproof and shockproof and designed for combat in water environments. Even their weapons had been upgraded to new machine guns that were mostly polymer, making them lighter and smaller. To a man, they had spent years of training learning to be invisible. They could move silently, kill quickly, navigate blindly and push their bodies way beyond normal endurance. A week in the swamp would sharpen them to a razor.

As they unpacked their crates of gear, Mackey walked to the edge of the old cracked runway and smiled. He had been here before, but it had been many years. Cascaes caught his gaze and asked him what was up.

"Been a while, Chris, but I've been here before. The original training courses were for operations in Cuba that never happened, then for Latin America. Actually did some work in Nicaragua after training here once many years ago. The swamp here is as nasty as it gets—until you get to the real one filled with people trying to kill you."

"Yeah, SEAL training was pretty rough, too. Funny how you think your instructor is trying to kill you until you are out working for real. Then you realize they taught you how to stay alive. How many times has some little trick from training saved our ass, huh?"

"Well, maybe this little excursion will be for nothing. If McKnight gets a green light for the FBI to go in and work with the Paraguayans, we'll be back off to the dessert again. That would be typical SNAFU—do jungle training in the river for a week, then ship out to the desert," said Mackey with a laugh.

"Yeah, no shit," said Cascaes with a laugh. "I remember doing training in Alaska for two weeks in the most miserable conditions of all time. I mean totally frozen, man. We were doing insertions from helicopters in zero viz, with winds blowing thirty knots at twenty below zero. The following week we were sneaking on to the beach in Iraq to take out some command and control targets in a desert. Typical." They both chuckled.

"Chief! We are good to go!" yelled Moose from the runway near the rear of the plane. The team had uncrated their gear and assembled themselves like a proper platoon.

Mackey looked back at them and smiled. "Chris, your guys are good. They've rubbed off on everybody else, too. Those guys from the Company—you think they ever stood at attention before?" He laughed out loud.

Mackey pulled his encrypted satellite phone from his breast pocket. He punched in the numbers for Dex Murphy's hotline and within a few seconds he had him on the line.

"Chief, jungle cruise is away at oh-six thirty. We are opening the mission pack now."

"Roger that, Tarzan. Check in at waypoint one. You have five hours. Over and out." With that, Dex hung up the phone.

Mackey and Cascaes opened the sealed mission pack and pulled out a small disc that they inserted into a miniature handheld computer. The computer, similar in size to a CD player, had a small color screen with GIS capabilities, as well as communication uplinks and a search and rescue homing beacon. Once the disc was in, Mackey tapped out his code, and a map of the area popped up. The first waypoint was shown in red down the Broad River approximately five miles downstream.

"Dex gave us five hours to go five miles. What am I missing?" asked Cascaes.

Mackey smiled. "The Glades here are unpredictable. Just because the river is shown someplace on the map, doesn't mean that's where it *is*. This place floods and changes course every season. If we're on the river, we can be there in twenty-five minutes. If we have to hump it carrying the rafts, I'm not sure we'll be there next week."

Cascaes smiled, his perfect white teeth gleaming in the hot sun. "The only easy day was yesterday, coach." He turned and started walking quickly to the men. "Okay boys! Vacation is over. We have five hours to cover five miles of nasty jungle. Temperature will go up ten degrees an hour, so I suggest we start humpin'. Move out!"

The men helped each other with the gear, including the inflatable rubber rafts that were the heaviest part of their equipment. The mean helped get the large deflated rafts, still in folded square bundles that weighed over sixty pounds, on to the backs of Moose and Ripper, who typically carried the heaviest loads. They strained under the weight as they found their centers of gravity. The packs weren't heavier than normal, just bulkier and harder to manage. Once everyone had their packs on, they followed Mackey and Cascaes single file into the misty heat of the glades.

An hour into their "walk in the woods," they realized why they had been given five hours. The trail ended only a few hundred yards away from the old airstrip and they found themselves in thorny vines and muck that tried to suck their boots off. Each step became slower than the last until they found a bearable pace in a huffing and puffing rhythm.

When they arrived at the point where the river should be, it wasn't there. Instead, they were struggling in muddy swamp and mangrove roots. They had all soaked through their jungle camos, and found themselves feeding the mosquitoes and flies. They stopped at the first fairly dry spot that they found and knelt down on one knee for a water break while Mackey and Cascaes decided their course of action. Mackey pulled out his computer and switched from the GPS map to a satellite image of their location. He kept zooming in until he could see exactly where they were supposed to be in real time, but of course the thick everglade canopy prevented them from seeing themselves. He moved around the screen trying to see in all directions for snakelike breaks in the canopy that might mean a river, but there wasn't much to go on. He eventually had to zoom out almost ten miles to find the Broad River where it became wider and more evident. Once he had located the river, he carefully backtracked to their present location, losing the tiny line along the way.

"At least we have a heading," he mumbled to Cascaes. "Send Santos and Jones ahead along this heading without their gear except for weapons, radio and GIS handheld. They're marine scouts and should be used to this shit."

Cascaes called them up and relayed the instructions. Santos and Jones stripped off their packs and quickly rubbed mosquito repellent all over their faces, necks and exposed arms and hands. They took a quick swig of water and hustled off into the thick tropical mess following the compass heading that Cascaes had given them. As marine scouts and eventually force recon marines, this was no worse than their usual playtime in the woods. Now, without sixty pounds of gear on their backs, they felt lighter, faster and more confident.

The rest of the team took a break for a quick MRE, water and a piss and waited for the two marines to radio in. They called in forty minutes later.

"Coach, this is shortstop. We're at the river. Over."

"How far from us, shortstop?" asked Mackey.

"Estimate another kilometer from where you are, but we have a better heading for you. We came the hard way. If you head north by northwest, you'll get to the river further upstream. We can insert there and float downstream. River looks deep enough and clear. Over."

"Roger, shortstop. Stay near the river and keep an eye out for us. We are en route."

"Roger that, coach. Oh, and one more thing, boss."

"Yeah?"

"There's fucking alligators out here. Out."

It was quiet enough in the swamp that they all heard what he said.

"Alligators? That's just great," mumbled Lance Woods, one of the Army Rangers.

Ripper, always one to bust chops took the shot. "Yeah, I know, Woods—you rangers always want to eat the local grub. You gonna eat gator, or gator gonna eat you?"

They re-shouldered their gear, plus the stuff left behind by Jones and Santos, and took off in the direction of their new heading. Jake Koches was on point with a machete, hacking his way through the nasty vines. Cascaes followed their progress on his handheld GPS system while Mackey kept his screen set on the satellite image. Thirty minutes later Lance Woods called back from his position on point that he could see the river ahead. It had been an hour and they hadn't covered a mile yet. They were all soaked with sweat and breathing like they had swum three miles.

Santos called in that he had visual and was heading in. They rendezvoused at the green slimy edge of the river and Ripper and Moose dropped the rafts on the mud. A quick press of a button and the two packs exploded into large black rafts each capable of holding eight men and equipment, although not particularly comfortably. In any case, it sure beat walking.

The men quietly stowed their gear in the rafts and assembled their small oars. The river had a slow current, but would do most of the work for them. They pushed into the stream and hopped in, straddling the sides of their rafts while drifting down the thick brownish green river. Birds called from everywhere, and occasionally a splash would alert them to an alligator entering the water.

As they continued downstream the brownish river became more like green water and less like brown liquefied mud. The current picked up ever so slightly and the sun shone down brightly on the men, lifting their spirits. The river meandered through the raw beauty that was the Everglades, and the men just took it all in. No one spoke as they watched birds flutter through the lush greenery. In less than twenty minutes they traveled three times as far as they had in the first hour, and they arrived at their first waypoint two hours ahead of schedule.

Once they were where they were supposed to be, the GIS indicator changed from red to green and popped up a new set of coordinates with their second waypoint. It was a delta where the Broad River met the Gulf, and that news brought big smiles to the SEALs.

"Boys, we are gonna be in crystal clear blue water this time tomorrow," announced Cascaes with a smile. That brought more than a few "hoo-aas," and an increase in the speed of the paddling.

CHAPTER 9

Jungles near Ciudad del Este, Paraguay

Vega was in a sour mood. Evidently, the little bitch had gone crying to Chief Kuka about Vega's "improprieties." Communication with Kuka was always a challenge, and it took a gift of one of Vega's machetes to calm the old man down. Kuka made reference to wanting rum, but Vega had made that mistake only once. The men were angry drunks, and it never took more than a few swigs for them to get out of control. In the end, the chief settled for the machete and Vega's half apology.

He and the chief headed out to the center of the village, where his men had assembled along with fifty of Kuka's porters and warriors. The warriors wore their green feathers and paint which, they were sure, made them invisible in the jungle. Vega's men all carried AK-47s, but had put extra ammunition, C-4, detonators and rocket launchers in a pile on the ground for the porters to carry for them on the long miserable walk back to the river in Brazil.

The Guarani women brought smoked meats and fish wrapped in leaves to their men for the journey. Vega's men would eat the same thing, although they brought their own water, treated with chlorine tablets. The Guarani men were happy to drink water from the ground, leaves, or holes in trees. Nothing seemed to make them sick, unlike Vega's men.

Enrique went over his instructions one last time with his three best men, and Kuka spoke with his own warriors and porters as well. They were all clear on their mission, and headed out into the jungle to the beautiful singing of the Guarani women and children.

They would walk the two days to the river where the Arabs had a boat waiting for them. The boat would take Vega's men, leaving the Guaranis to wait for their return. Vega's men would continue north to the great Itaipu Dam, then disembark to waiting trucks that would drive them to Ciudad del Este. Once there, they had maps and specific instructions on what was to occur and when.

⊕

Leah was with Director Holstrum and Darren Davis in the director's office when she called down to her agent in Paraguay on an encrypted phone. The conference call had been arranged the day before, as it wasn't always easy for Julia Ortiz to get total privacy. She had a small office on the outskirts of Ciudad del Este in the International Center for Domestic Relief. Her office, which employed locals to work with the Guaranis, was usually empty because they would typically be out in the field working with the indigenous people to help them find employment, improve their education and improve their housing.

The CIA funded a good portion of their efforts through paper charities, which actually *did* help the Guaranis, but ultimately, that wasn't the actual mission. Julia Ortiz, who was as beautiful as any Hollywood model, used her position as the director of the center to gain access to as many of Paraguay's influential politicians as possible. While they considered her a lobbyist and general "do-gooder" with her hand out for funds, Paraguay's most powerful politicians were always eager to speak with her and have their photos taken with the "Guardian of the Guaranis".

The poor of Paraguay considered her a saint, and the poor voted, too. It was always in the politician's best interest to remain on her good side. Almost every one of the men she came in contact with propositioned her, some more blatantly than others. Two members of the Council of Ministers, the president's direct Cabinet, had actually come right out and told her that they would get her more funding if she would agree to a few days in their private villas. The "Latin lovers" had no success, however, she did continue to flirt shamelessly with them. Even when working in the field, her short black hair and huge brown eyes shone like polished ebony. She had high cheekbones and a golden complexion, the type that millions of Americans paid for under UV lamps.

At five feet tall and a hundred pounds, you'd think she would blend into her surroundings, but it was not the case. Wherever she went, she was noticed. At first, it was assumed she could never be a field agent because of that simple fact, until she learned how to use it to her advantage. Her smile and pleading eyes opened doors that others simply could not. She had learned to love the Guarani people over the few years she had been there, and her cover story ended up being a passion of hers. She was doing not only high quality work gathering intelligence on the Paraguayan government, but also for the poor natives that had been so abused for the past five-hundred years. After three years with them, she had actually become fairly fluent in their ancient language—something not easily done, since it didn't resemble Spanish or Portuguese at all.

For the sake of the incoming call, she had made sure her staff was busy and out of her small office. She swept it for bugs using equipment supplied by the CIA as she did before each phone call, and locked herself in her small office.

"Hello, Julia," said Leah from a world away. "I am here with the director and another friend. We're checking in to see if there's anything new floating around the rumor mill."

"Hello my friends," she said quietly. "Do you refer to our friend Jim's arrival?"

"Yes. We understand he has a meeting with the vice-president to discuss handling some problems in the jungle. Do you have any predictions on his success?"

"I do not know the vice-president myself," she said. "But, if he is anything like the President's Cabinet or the senators and deputies I have met, our friend Jim had better be bringing a suitcase."

"Do you think it goes that high?" asked Leah.

"Nothing would surprise me here. Sometimes I think about these Latin and South American countries and I want to cry. They're full of natural resources and people that want to work, and yet they all live in poverty except for the elite. It's a disgrace. I have yet to find a politician down here that really cares about anything other than his own bank account and staying elected."

"Makes the States looks a little better?" asked Leah.

"You have no idea. Sometimes I can't wait to get the hell out of here, and then other days the Guarani children will teach me a song or take me for a walk through the forest and I could stay here forever. Anyway, there's only so much one person can do down here."

"Well, we all hear you are doing great things for the locals. I don't think we've ever had one of our employees take their extra employment so seriously. You are to be commended. Julia, can you get a feel for what is happening in the tri-border area now?"

"I haven't heard much since my last report to you, really. Vega appears to have wiped out all of his competitors, and the rumors about weapons coming in from the Middle East are almost common knowledge. I had mentioned that to a senator last month—about the fact that Guaranis shouldn't be carrying AK-47s, and he laughed at me. 'They aren't the ones with the AKs,' he told me, like that was supposed to make me feel better. The local Guaranis tell me that Vega employs Pampidos Guaranis that have returned to the jungle and the ancient ways. They are *fierce* people. I've heard rumors of cannibalism, although I have no proof."

"How lovely," said Leah. "We understand that there are plenty of Iranians and Arabs living in Ciudad del Este now—true?"

"Yes. This is an industrial and international city. The crime rate is horrible, and yet foreign nationals keep coming here. I am pretty damn sure that Al Qaeda, Hamas, and Hezbollah all have plenty of representation down here. And they all have deep pockets, which is why I am doubtful that Jim will have much success. I don't think it's any secret that he is here to pressure the Paraguayan government to help go after these organizations."

Director Holstrum spoke up. "Julia, this is the director. First off, you are doing a great job—I mean that. I hope you will stay down there a while longer."

"Yes, sir, thank you," she said quietly.

"In the event that Jim can't get our friends to play along nicely down there, we do have a 'Plan B.' You will be contacted should this go into effect. Your knowledge of the Guarani people and the lay of the land down there will be important should it come to that."

"Visitors, sir?" she asked.

"Affirmative," he said.

"With all respect, you'd need a small army, sir," she said.

"We agree with you, Julia. And that is exactly what we intend to use."

CHAPTER 10

Ciudad del Este

The Guaranis led Vega's men through the winding jungle trails back to the river where the boats where waiting for them. To an outsider, it might seem strange to see an Iranian crew aboard a boat in Paraguay greeting a group of green painted warriors and drug smugglers. But it was just another day on the Parana River.

The Guaranis loaded the boat and then disappeared back into the jungle to await the return of Vega's men. As soon as the boat was loaded and Vega's men were all aboard, the crew gunned the engine and they roared upstream towards to world's largest dam.

It was a pleasant ride for Vega's men, with the air blowing over them at thirty-five knots—a welcomed change from the sticky and stagnant air of the jungle. They disembarked at their waiting trucks and reloaded, then set off up the dirt roads that would lead to the highways going to Ciudad del Este. They arrived at night, and began scrambling around in the dark city streets, preparing for a morning that would rock the city and send a message to the Americans about meddling in their part of the world.

⊕

Ambassador Jim McKnight sat in the back of a black SUV following his security detail. A second SUV followed close behind with his secretary and another staff member. In all, there were eleven of them in the three sleek black vehicles. It was almost nine in the morning. Jim had gotten up at six and went over his speech one last time, the one he would give to the twenty other nations that would be attending the summit. More importantly, he planned to share proof with the vice president about Middle Eastern involvement in the local drug trade and weapons trafficking. He had been called by the US President himself two days ago to remind him of the importance of this diplomatic mission. McKnight was a veteran of the diplomatic corps and a good negotiator. If anyone could get it done, it was he.

As their small convoy approached the Paraguayan Center for International Trade, traffic slowed. Hundreds of vehicles with diplomatic tags filled the streets and television news crews were setting up near the large steps that led to the massive granite columns outside the impressive building. Police and private security teams stood around with machine guns across their chests, a show of force that was just that—a show.

McKnight's convoy came to a stop behind the Brazilian convoy, which was cued up behind the Mexican convoy that was already unloading. McKnight was shoving his papers into his valise when Vega's man Carlos pressed the button on the detonator from across the street. The C-4 that had been carefully hidden with bags of gutter nails in ten large flower pots near the entranceway went off simultaneously, sending the Mexican Ambassador's Mercedes ten feet into the air and, like a claymore mine, sending out a cloud of thousands of nails.

While the windows of McKnight's SUV where instantly blown out, his aide's body absorbed the nails and glass, shielding McKnight enough to save his life, though he was rendered unconscious. One of Carlos's men made sure he wouldn't last long though. From the bushes in the small park across the square, he fired a rocket at the damaged vehicle. As bodies were still landing from the first explosion, the rocket whooshed through the air, scoring a direct hit on McKnight's vehicle. The armor-piercing round sent his truck into the air in a giant fireball, killing everyone inside instantly. A second rocket hit the truck behind him with similar results, a split second before another of Carlos's men set off the second and largest charge by the front doors. Anyone on the street that was running towards the building for cover was blown off their feet in a cloud of fire and nails.

Almost every vehicle on the street was either completely destroyed, or burning and unable to move. There wasn't a person left standing anywhere near the building. Carlos's team in the park dropped the missile launchers and ran to their waiting car. Carlos dropped the detonator into a small trashcan as he walked quickly away from the commotion. Anyone nearby was dead, wounded, or running for their life, and as Carlos's team disappeared into the chaos, not one person took notice of them. Carlos smiled at the sound of sirens heading towards the chaos. They were out of the city and heading towards the boats before the first ambulance arrived on the scene.

CHAPTER 11

Director Holstrum's phone was ringing less than five minutes after McKnight and his entire entourage had been assassinated. News of the event was delayed several minutes because most of the film crews were also killed in the explosion.

Meanwhile, Raman, Hakim, and Ali had been sitting by a television in an Argentinean coffee shop hoping to watch the explosion live. Instead, they had to settle for "breaking news alerts" followed by coverage of the scene after the attack, since none of the cameras that had been filming survived the blasts.

The devastation on the street was obvious. Black smoke still clung over the burning vehicles, which were nothing more than twisted metal. Body parts and charred remains were evident in the media coverage, but hard news about those attacked was sketchy since identifications would take days, weeks, or perhaps could never be accomplished at all. Witnesses were being interviewed by news commentators and local police investigators, but no one had seen much other than the huge explosions. Police were finding nails imbedded in walls all the way across the park, and the number of injured was now well over three hundred. The two closest hospitals were completely overwhelmed and were doing triage outside in the parking lot.

Ali Aziz stroked his long beard and smiled slowly. "It would appear that Señor Vega performed even beyond our hopes. Still no word on the Americans, but I am sure he did not disappoint us."

Raman sipped his tea and watched the television. The reporter answered Ali's question as though she had heard him. She was standing with her back to ambulances and rescue personnel on the blackened street.

"The latest word, which is still unconfirmed, is that the entire Mexican, Brazilian, and American delegations were annihilated in this morning's attack. Investigators are asking witnesses to please come forward with any information that may help them piece together what has happened this morning on this once-quiet street. So far, no one has claimed responsibility, and speculation about the attack has been conflicting and varied..."

The reporter held her earpiece and listened for a second, then began speaking again. "I am told now that it *is* confirmed—US Ambassador James McKnight and his entire staff were killed, along with Mexican Ambassador Juan Concepcione and his delegation as well. Still no official word on the Brazilian contingent, however, a license plate from their vehicle *has* been identified..."

Raman put his cup down and looked at Hakim. He slid a disposable cell phone to him across the table. "You have a phone call to make. Read the script exactly as written—it is under thirty seconds. Then destroy the phone, remove the battery, and throw it in the water. We'll meet back at the hotel and then off to the airport. By this time tomorrow, we will be celebrating with our people in Syria."

Back in Virginia, the director was standing in front of a bank of televisions with Leah and Darren. Leah was listening to the live reports in Spanish and occasionally translating something of interest to Darren and Wallace, who were watching FOX and CNN simultaneously. Holstrum's phone ran again. He answered it and then did more listening than speaking. He hung up and sat on his desk with his arms folded.

"That was the Secretary of Defense. The president has called for Plan B." Director Holstrum looked sad, an adjective that wouldn't normally fit his persona.

"You okay, boss?" asked Darren.

He shook his head slowly, then took off his glasses and wiped his tired eyes. "I've known Jim McKnight for almost ten years. I was at his daughter's wedding for Christ's sake." He stood up and put his glasses back on, shoving his hands in his pockets and walking to the window. Leah and Darren gave him a second to himself.

"Where are your boys, Darren?" he asked.

"Training in Florida, sir. They're out in the Everglades. It will take a day or two to get them back," Darren replied.

"Bring 'em in. The faster the better. Leah, reach out to every contact you have south of the border and start shaking the trees. We have a green light to start tracing this attack, and if I'm right, the trail will lead back Al Qaeda working in the tri-border region. This is now priority one." Holstrum walked back to his large desk and sat down, looking devastated. "I have to call Jim's wife."

Leah and Darren looked at each and then excused themselves to allow the director some privacy.

"Leah, let's meet in my situation room in an hour. Bring whoever is going to be working with you on this. We need to start working out details ASAP," said Darren.

"One hour," she replied, and the two of them took off down the hall in opposite directions.

CHAPTER 12

The Glades

The members of the team had found the driest place they could to stop for the night. The pulled their rafts ashore and hiked up to a small clearing where they flipped the rafts upside down and placed them on the thick grass. Cascaes inspected the area carefully for alligator nests, mindful not to invite trouble of the reptilian kind. The men pulled out green mosquito nets that were like personal cocoons. They would sleep on top of the upside-down rafts—cramped but dry and off the ground that was crawling with who knows what.

They built two small fires using sterno packs to help light the damp wood and then ate their MREs. Lance Woods drew first watch, which would last until two A.M., then Moose would take over until four, and finally Hodges until daybreak. The men finished eating and went over the day's adventures, then started looking at their computer equipment and satellite images to try and find themselves on the river. The technology was amazing, and after a few minutes of tinkering, they could actually see the lights of their fires on the screen. They were being seen from a satellite thousands of miles away, and yet could focus down through the swamps to see their small campfires.

"Yo, man," said Ernie P. with a smile. "Why don't you change those coordinates to Daytona, man. See if you can get some pussy on that thing! There's gotta' be some chick laying outside naked *someplace!*"

"No, man," said Raul Santos, "If you're gonna change coordinates, take a look at some place where the sun is still up! Grab a picture of the beach in Hawaii, man!"

Everyone chuckled. Mackey, being the old man of the group, felt compelled to keep his group serious. "You are supposed to be training in the jungle, not whacking off looking at chicks a thousand miles away. Now leave your peckers alone and get some sleep."

The joking continued for another hour, and then one by one the men began zipping up inside their nets and sacking out on the rafts. By midnight, everyone was asleep except for Lance, who was on watch. Mackey woke up after catching an hour and a half of sleep. He hated sleeping in the jungle—something left over from his Vietnam memories, and got up. He unzipped the top part of his net and let his head stick out, and walked over the fire where Lance was sitting drinking coffee.

Lance whispered, "What's up, boss? Everything okay?"

"Yeah, everything's fine. I'll take your watch. Go get some sleep."

"You sure? I have until two..."

Mackey smacked his arm and told him to go ahead and sleep. Lance was out cold in five minutes, a talent that most of these guys possessed from years of never knowing when you would be able to sleep. Mackey sat quietly and made some coffee, stirring the fire with a long stick. He eventually began to hear Earl Jones sniffling and mumbling to himself. When he looked over to the raft, Jones got up and walked to one of the other small fires. Mackey followed him over and squatted down next to him. Jones had tears running down his face.

"What's up, Jonesy?" asked Mackey.

"Nuthin', coach, I'm fine."

"Bullshit, man. You still having nightmares?"

Jonesy looked at him with an expression of surprise. "Santos dime me out?"

"Look man, don't get on Santos. It was his responsibility to tell me if there was a problem somewhere—just like it would yours if the situation was reversed. You get distracted with shit in the field and people get killed, Earl." Mackey was talking slightly above a whisper.

"I'm fine, coach. Just some nightmares is all," said Jones quietly. He wiped his face with the back of his hand.

"Tell me about them," said Mackey.

Jones just looked at him for a second. He was afraid to open his mouth lest he start crying uncontrollably again.

"Not much to tell," he said quietly. "I just see those kids, man. Two little fucking kids I killed."

Mackey scowled. I know how you feel inside, Jonesy. But you gotta' let it go, man…"

"I've been *trying*, man!" he said. "I try and block it out, but those kids just keep popping back into my head. It's every fucking night, man. I can't sleep…"

"Look, Earl—I'm going to tell you something that very few people on this planet know, but maybe it will help. Just shut up and listen for a second." Mackey looked back at the rafts to make sure everyone was still sleeping.

"When I was in Vietnam, I did mostly flying. Reconnaissance stuff. I'd fly around and spot enemy locations, take pictures, and fly home. Not sure how many people my snapshots killed, but I bet it was plenty. Anyway, towards the end of my tour, my plane got shot to shit and I had to make an emergency landing. My co-pilot had been killed, and I force landed near a small village about five klicks from our base. Luckily for me, it was starting to get dark, and as soon as I hit the ground I grabbed Steve's dog tags, said goodbye and apologized for leaving his ass out in the fucking jungle. I ran as fast as I could through the jungle towards home.

Sometime in the middle of the night, I came across a hut. I saw a guy in black pajamas outside of it with his back to me and I was sure he was VC. I was scared shitless, man. I was nineteen and used to being *above* the jungle, not in it. So I snuck up behind this guy, and not wanting to risk any noise, I put my hand over his mouth and slit his throat with my Ka-Bar knife, then stabbed him another hundred times out of total fear. When I flipped him over, he wasn't a VC soldier, he was a little kid—maybe thirteen years old. Ya' see, the dinks were small people…in the dark, I couldn't have known. Anyway, that kid's eyes were wide open. So was his mouth. And he was just staring at me, like he was asking me why I killed him."

"Shit," said Earl quietly.

"Yeah. Shit. I started running again. Running and crying for hours. It's a wonder I didn't step on a mine or trigger a booby trap or attract a whole fucking company of gooks. But somehow, for some stupid reason, I made it back to our base. And then that kid started visiting me every night just like your two friends."

Earl just sat staring at him, glossy eyed. "How long did it last?"

"Only about twenty years," said Mackey, watching Earl's face fall. "But it doesn't have to be that way for you."

"What do you mean?" he asked.

"Well, twenty years after I came home, I was still seeing that kid every night. I eventually did what I should have done twenty years earlier and went to a shrink about my 'post traumatic stress disorder,' as she called it."

Earl just sat listening, hopeful that something Mackey would say could save his soul.

Mackey cleared his throat. "Anyway, I told her the whole story—not just the Reader's Digest version you just got. Then she asked me the damndest thing."

"What was that?" asked Earl.

"She asked me if I ever apologized to him." He let that hang in the air for a while. "See, I knew I didn't mean to kill him, it was an accident. But I felt that guilt for twenty years and it almost wasted me, man. So anyway, a few nights later, the kid was back in my nightmare—except *this* time, I *apologized*."

Earl could feel tears running down his face again and didn't bother wiping them. "So what happened?" he managed to choke out.

"I apologized and the kid understood. And after that, he never came back. I was a free man. Anyway—you might try it. When those kids come back to visit you—you talk to them. Tell 'em it was an accident. Apologize to them; make friends with them—*something*. You gotta' find some peace with it, Earl, and let it go. And if you can't, you have to tell me and I will send you someplace to get some help. Don't do what I did and let it eat you up inside for twenty years, okay?"

Earl shook his head yes and wiped his face. Mackey smacked him on the back. "Now go get some sleep. The only easy day was yesterday." He smiled, and Earl smiled back, some of the stress having left his face. He stood up and started walking over to the raft.

"Hey, Mack," he called out quietly. Mackey turned to him. "Thanks, man."

CHAPTER 13

Sunrise, in the Glades

Mackey had finally fallen asleep around three, and three hours later, the sounds of the Everglades began waking him back up again. The birds were screaming bloody murder from every direction, and bugs where buzzing all around in giant annoying clouds. Hodges was sitting by the fire making coffee for everyone. He looked at his watch and sang out.

"Okay ladies! It's oh-six hundred! Coffee is made but you'll have to find your own doughnuts!"

The team was groaning from the rafts, each man trying to untangle himself from his mosquito net and stand up. As they stood up, Santos laughed.

"Yo! Jonesy! Shake and bake, baby!" yelled Santos.

Mackey was groggy, but realized that Earl was still fast asleep. Maybe he had finally gotten a few real hours of peace. Mackey smiled to himself and stood up stretching his aching back.

Jones woke up and looked around, totally confused at first. And then, for the first time since Saudi, he smiled his warm relaxed grin that always made everyone around him smile. He looked over at Mackey and mouthed, "thank you".

Cascaes was up and grabbing coffee as the team packed up their nets and reorganized themselves. Most of them found a moment of privacy in the bushes for their personal business.

Cascaes popped the computer on and checked to see their new waypoint. Much to his surprise, the computer screen came up reading "Training mission aborted. Contact base immediately."

"Holy shit, coach. Something's up." He showed the screen to Mackey.

Mackey sighed. "Never a dull moment." He unpacked the satellite phone and set up the encrypted call to Dex Murphy. Murphy answered immediately.

"Manager, this is the coach. Got a funny message this morning—what's up?"

"Nothing funny about it. Where are you?"

"In the middle of the fucking swamp where you put me, what the hell's going on?"

"I mean *exactly*, where are you?"

Mackey relayed the question to Cascaes, who plotted their location and read off the coordinates to Mackey, who relayed them back to Dex. Dex mumbled a "shit" when he saw where they were on his map.

"Alright, get back on the river and move as fast as you can downstream. I will try and arrange your pickup and bring you back up here."

"Does that mean that McKnight didn't have much luck in Paraguay?" asked Mackey.

"Mack—McKnight is dead, along with his entire staff. So are the Mexican and Brazilian Ambassadors, along with a few hundred civilians. Paraguay TV is saying that they received a call from Al Qaeda claiming responsibility, and promising more attacks if America doesn't get out of Iraq and Afghanistan. The president has authorized Plan B. That's *you*. I need you back in Langley, ASAP. If you hustle downstream, we can get a seaplane to pick you up and bring you directly here. Turn on your emergency homing beacon and we'll track you from here as you move west. We'll be in touch as soon as a plane is en route. Over and out."

Mackey activated the homing beacon. In an instant, their little handheld computer was bouncing signals off of a satellite directly to CIA's main computer system. Handlers inside the agency could track their every move while sitting in Virginia.

Mackey called out to his team. "Okay boys, on me!" The team sensed the change in his demeanor and trotted over to him immediately.

"I just received word from Langley that the US Ambassador to Paraguay and his entire staff were assassinated. That means that we're going to be playing in the jungle for real. This training exercise is over as of *right now*. We are ordered to proceed downriver ASAP where a seaplane will be waiting to pick us up. That's all I have for you right now. Everybody hustle up."

The team immediately sprang into action, flipping the rafts and filling them with all of their gear, then running them down to the river. The men ignored the large alligator sunning itself on the bank and piled into the raft. Within a few minutes from hanging up the phone, the two rafts were heading downstream at their fastest pace yet.

CHAPTER 14

Eastern Paraguay

Vega's men drove quickly out of the city and headed back to the river where their Iranian crew was anchored and waiting for them, greeting them with big smiles. While the crew hadn't been told anything, the Iranians weren't stupid, and assumed correctly that these men had carried out the attack that was all over the news.

They moved quickly down river to where the Iranians had originally picked them up, and the Iranians dropped them all off there again. The Iranians roared off after they had unloaded their passengers, waving and smiling proudly as they disappeared upriver.

As if by magic, the Guarani warriors began emerging from the woods. They just appeared, without making a sound. Vega's men had no gear to carry anymore, having used it all in the attack. They had ditched their AK-47s when they left the city in case they were stopped, but no matter, there were plenty more back at Vega's camp.

Vega's men followed the Guaranis back into the jungle, stopping every now and then to send a few Guaranis back down the trail and make sure they weren't being followed. When they were satisfied that they had gotten away cleanly, they moved quickly through the jungle towards "home."

The warriors arrived back in the village, leading their tired terrorists, to the sounds of singing and celebration. The Guarani women and children were playing drums, flutes and primitive instruments, and singing their beautiful songs. Vega walked out of his hut smoking a cigar and smiling. He gave the warriors blankets as gifts to bring home to their families and invited his men back to his hut for rum and smokes.

Vega expressed his thanks to the abrubicha and left the celebration as the families celebrated being reunited after the five-day trip. The natives would continue their singing and dancing for hours, and it got on Vega's nerves after a while. His men followed him back to his hut where they drank rum and smoked and filled Vega in on the events of the journey. As the Arabs had promised, it went smoothly. There had been no unpleasant surprises and no one had seen them. No one alive, anyway.

They finished getting drunk and the discussion turned to the differences between Guarani breasts and the women they knew back home. This led to more graphic discussions, of course, and finally Vega decided his men really *did* deserve a reward for carrying out the mission as well as they did. He grabbed a bottle of rum, against his better judgment, and decided to go find Kuka to try and arrange a business transaction—a bottle of rum for a half dozen Guarani women for the evening. It was a tricky proposal. Kuka could be funny about that sometimes. While "prostitution" didn't exist in Guarani culture, the chief did understand the concept of trading, and being a horny old bugger himself, didn't begrudge Vega for wanting his women. The tricky part was making sure that Kuka was properly compensated. To offer him too little would be a serious insult, and Vega, although always ready to get laid, knew that his business dealings with the Guarani came first. Kuka and his warriors loved getting drunk, but it had led to problems in the past and almost got one of his men killed. This time Vega would be wiser. He had watered down the rum to half-strength.

Vega told his men to wait in the hut, and set off back to the center of the village where the celebration continued. With a bottle of rum, even watered down, it was about to get a lot rowdier. Vega chuckled out loud as he spotted the chief and began thinking about his present life. It wasn't bad really, except for the miserable humidity and thick jungle air that was filled with bugs. Kuka might have *thought* he was the chief, but Vega laughed again as decided *he* was king of the jungle. Another couple of years of this, and would buy his own island in the Caribbean and live like a *real* king.

CHAPTER 15

Langley

Darren Davis and Dex Murphy sat in the situation room with Leah Pereira and a member of her staff. They would be calling Julia Ortiz down in Paraguay later in the day, but had lots to discuss before then.

They had been drinking coffee and floating out ideas about the insertion of the team for about twenty minutes, but every idea was flawed. Dozens of scenarios were discussed ranging from HALO jumps into the jungle (for which only the SEALs and rangers were qualified) to a baseball game in Brazil or Argentina. As the group "brainstormed" through a dozen more ideas, they kept coming back to Julia in Paraguay.

Landing openly in Paraguay was out—the Paraguayan government was scared shitless of more terrorist activity, and openly called for the US to get out of the Middle East, as if *that* was going to end terrorism in the world. They had flatly turned down the US request to send a team of FBI investigators down after the terrorist attack. They told the State Department that they would handle it themselves using their best people and promised that those responsible would be brought to justice. The FBI was outraged, but was told to "stand down" by the president—there were other options being considered. This was now the other option.

Leah called Julia on her encrypted phone and she picked up right away. The conversation ended up lasting almost an hour. In the end, it was decided to use the team, but scrap the baseball cover story. The timing just didn't seem right after such a large terrorist attack. Instead, they would get into Paraguay in small groups, pairs or individually as volunteers for Julia's outreach program with the Guaranis. CIA would make new cover stories, names and documents for the team members. Julia had suggested a church group for moving a larger group in at one time, complete with bad T-Shirts, which actually seemed like a plausible idea.

For the equipment and weapons, it was a little more complicated. The US carrier fleets were deployed all over the world—except for anywhere near South America. Ideally, they would have transported the gear by plane to a nearby aircraft carrier for transfer to a sub that could ferry the weapons and ammo for an offshore handoff. With no carriers in the area, they would instead have to fly to a point off the coast of Brazil and drop the gear into the ocean, where a waiting sub would pick it up and then sneak in closer to shore where it could be transferred to the team. Which would have been fine if the target was in eastern Brazil instead of Paraguay. A river trip with a boatload of high-tech spy equipment and weapons was not plausible. Back to square one.

Julia piped up from her end, sounding like the chipper young lady she was, "I get two shipments in a month, minimum, depending on funding. Connex containers come in from Santos. With seventy million tons of freight coming in every year, they don't check very carefully. I have been going with my drivers for so long now that they don't even look at the manifest anymore."

Darren and Leah looked at each and shrugged while raising their eyebrows.

"Might work," said Darren.

"It *will* work. The Connex containers are forty feet long. They come off the ship by crane and are slapped on the back of a tractor-trailer. They rarely inspect them. Can you fit what you need in the front twenty feet of the container—a space twenty by eight feet and eight feet high? Then we could pack the *rear* half with *normal* supplies. Even if they opened the container at the port or searched the truck later on, they'd never unload the whole thing."

"That's more than enough," said Darren. "Our team travels fairly light." He paused and squinted.

"What are you thinking?" asked Leah.

"It's more than enough room. Wouldn't be a pleasant trip, but it is another way in for team members."

Julia piped up from her end. "Forget it, unless you are packing an air conditioner in there and you really hate the guys that work for you. It would take a few days and would be over a hundred degrees in there. You'd roast your men."

"No refrigeration onboard?" Darren asked.

"No, we get mostly canned goods, medical supplies, dehydrated food stuffs that can take heat, plus some clothing. And the occasional packages *you* send me." She was referring to cash, documents and whatever else CIA needed to get to her. They usually were sent sealed inside boxes of tampons. Only once had the container been checked, and the macho security officer had been embarrassed in front of pretty Julia when he saw what the box was. He went past it as fast as he could and then tried for the fifth time to make idle chatter with Julia. No luck.

"Okay, so that's out then—just thinking out loud. But I like the container idea. Is there a set schedule?" Darren asked.

Leah answered for Julia. "Not really. She has fairly standard shipments, but they often get held up until the ship is fully loaded. No one would notice a change in delivery date."

"She's right," confirmed Julia. You can send it down right away. It will still take at least a week. Can your team be down here by then?"

Darren looked at Leah and rolled his eyes. "Not sure yet. At this particular moment my men are running around the Everglades. We are trying to get them back ASAP. Then we need to document them and brief them. A week seems awfully fast."

Leah smacked his arm, a gesture uncharacteristic of her genteel and professional nature. "They can do it, Darren. No problem. We'll have them here in thirty-six hours, briefed and set up with new docs in another twenty-four, and en route to Julia immediately after they know where they are going. Can you get the gear list together today?"

Darren wiped his face with his hands, feeling stressed again. "Okay—I can put the mission together with you that fast assuming we get our team back here in a day and a half, but I need to speak to Mackey and Cascaes about the gear. They have trained on our latest and greatest, but they still prefer some of their own stuff, especially when it comes to weapons. They are a hybrid outfit—it gets a little complicated."

"Okay, so get a message off to them, ask them what they need, and we'll put it together as they fly back. If they have to wait a day or two for the gear to arrive, it wouldn't be the worst thing. I'm sure Julia could use the help down there."

Julia laughed from her end of the phone. "If you send me ten strong guys, I'll have a new school built in a week."

"You won't have a week. If we fly the Connex to Puerto Rico, they can load it aboard ship there and save a couple of days. Julia, when was the last time you had volunteers down there, arriving at your place, I mean?" Said Leah.

"You mean real ones?" asked Julia. She had often had CIA agents or other agency's personnel go through her as a cover.

"Yeah, real ones. Ever have a large group show up down there?" asked Leah.

"A few times, actually. Couple of church groups, Peace Corps one time, and then local groups down here, too."

"How large were the groups?" she asked.

"Peace Corps sent twenty, and they stayed about a month to build the water purifier. One church group was about ten, the other was big, like thirty. They didn't stay as long, though.

They were touring Central and South America. I know where you are going with this. It would be safe, Leah. You could send the whole crew into Brazil. Have them meet up with us at the port. Maybe throw in some lumber and building supplies. We can say they are building me my schoolhouse."

"Damn—she really wants that school," said Darren with a smile.

"I really do, actually," she said. "But it would also be a perfect cover. If there aren't any females in your crew, then make them a church group of volunteer construction workers. I've been promising a school for over a year."

"So now I need to add lumber and nails to my list, too?" asked Darren. The director is going to love this request."

"Quit your bitching," said Leah. "I happen to know that you have some spending money right now." She flashed her sexy smile.

Darren was surprised that she knew about the truck that had been taken down in Saudi Arabia by the team a few weeks prior. He didn't acknowledge her comment. "I'll see what I can do," was all he said.

Leah told Julia that they would be in touch again within thirty-six hours. She hung up and looked at Darren. "We can ship the container into Santos and fly the men in there all together. It's a little over five hundred miles from Santos to Paraguay. They can make the trip in a day, albeit a long one. The roads get a little hairy near the border."

"And the border crossing into Paraguay? You think my team is going to just walk in at the border in one large group and not raise suspicion?"

"Why would they? Because of their haircuts? They'll be conservative Christians on a mission to help the natives. We'll do the bad t-shirts and everything. Julia is well known at the border. The locals love her down there. And I am serious about helping her with the school. We do enough 'wet work' in this office. How about a little redemption for us, too?" Leah was serious, and folded her hands to let everyone know she was done.

Darren looked at Dex and chucked his chin at him, as if to ask his opinion.

"Look, boss—if we were landing in Iran, I'd have an opinion. I have no idea how it works south of the border. If Leah and Julia are cool with it, I defer to them."

Leah's assistant, who hadn't said a word the entire meeting, but had been taking furious notes, finally spoke up. She was a sixty-year-old woman, a bit on the frumpy side, and made Leah look even better than she would have normally. "She knows South America," was all she said.

"Okay. Then that's our plan. I will hand off the shopping list to you, Dex. Leah—can you handle the lumber and construction supplies? You have a blueprint for this school of yours?"

She laughed. "This isn't America. No blueprints—nothing fancy. They want a roof and a floor. Maybe some benches. This isn't going to be ADA approved or pass local inspection. These people have *nothing*, Darren. But putting up a school for the local Guaranis will go a long way in building good will down there. And trust me, we need it."

CHAPTER 16

Western Everglades

Mackey and Cascaes sat next to each other in the bow of the first boat. They were monitoring the GPS handheld navigational computers and speaking with a pilot a couple of hundred miles away heading to their emergency homing beacon. The others rowed strong, silent and steady, practicing for the unknown. The SEALs had an easier time with the rowing, something they had all been doing for many years, and divided themselves between the two boats. They quietly coached and taught the others little tricks to extend the amount of time their arms would last pulling themselves through the water. They practiced controlled breathing, exhaling slowly as they pulled, and inhaling as they reached for the next scoop of green water. As arm-weary as they were, no one complained. The training mission, however brief, was over and now, even though they were in Florida, they were on a real mission, and were in serious mode.

As the paddled, they watched the mysterious world around them, each lost in his own thoughts. Deep in the Everglades like this, they had stepped back a few hundred years into American history and the days of Spanish exploration into the New World. They couldn't help but sense the foreshadowing of this expedition as they prepared to follow those Spanish explorers all the way to South America. Their thoughts were occasionally broken by the screeching of birds or splash of something around their boat. At least no one was shooting at them.

Cascaes turned to face the rear of the boat, and could easily speak to the other boat directly behind them. "Listen up, people!"

No one stopped paddling, but faced their second in command.

"We are still pretty far from the Gulf, but in about three miles, the river gets wider and straight enough to land the seaplane. Most likely, our ride will be sitting out there waiting for us when we get there. We'll load up and scuttle the rafts. Then straight back to Langley for a full briefing and mission planning. In less than three days, we will most likely be in Brazil or Paraguay paddling, just like you are right now, except there may be a few folks wandering around who don't appreciate us being there. This evac will be good practice, so hit it like it's the real deal. Move quickly and efficiently and let's get that bird off the water as fast as possible. Nobody goes swimming, okay? Any questions?"

Ripper, who had been in the rear of the first boat and been quietly acting as the coxswain sang out a "no questions, Skipper—now let's *move!*" He increased the speed of the rowing, the other boat stepping up into the rhythm. The men were already soaked with sweat, but now felt a change in the urgency, and enjoyed the slight adrenaline rush as they started rowing like a well trained crew-team.

The two boats glided through the thick green water, now oblivious to the wildlife and beauty around them. They concentrated on their breathing and the voice of Ripper as he quietly kept them in their focused rhythm. It was almost an hour of intense rowing before they heard the seaplane's engine far in the distance. A few minutes later Mackey's radio squawked and the pilot came back on reporting that "their ride was waiting." The men kept their intense pace, and as they came around a little bend in the river, the river opened much wider and straightened out to reveal the large seaplane anchored in the center of the river.

As they spotted the plane, its door opened and a crewman stepped out onto the pontoon, waving at their arriving passengers. The first boat glided in next to the pontoon and the team immediately began working. Cascaes was up first, jumping on to the pontoon and holding the bow of the raft along with the air crewman, who held the aft. The men worked silently and quickly, moving every item aboard the plane and then themselves hopping out. Ripper, in the stern, pulled out his Ka-Bar knife and popped off a protected cover to reveal a cap that read "Emergency Scuttle." He twisted the knob, then punched a few holes into the floor of the raft to speed up the quick process. The Emergency Scuttle had already activated two very small ballast tanks which flooded immediately. By the time he stepped on to the pontoon and followed the others inside the plane, his raft was already disappearing under the green water.

Moose repeated the process as the last man out of the second boat, and then quickly hopped aboard the plane. As large as it looked empty, the plane was quickly cramped with men and gear. The pilot stepped back from his seat and greeted the men, complimenting them on their extremely quick transfer from boat to plane. They pulled up their anchor, taxied slowly to the end of their little straightaway, then revved the engines and hydroplaned until they took off, turning north.

⊕

It took two and a half hours for the seaplane to make it to the private strip in Langley, landing on its wheels which were imbedded under the pontoons. The men piled out quickly and reassembled their gear neatly beside the runway as the black bus arrived to bring them back to their building. Dex Murphy was on the bus with them, having greeted them at the strip as soon as he arrived with the bus.

"Nothing personal guys, but your first order of business is the shower. Y'all smell pretty damn ripe."

Raul Santos, one of the marines smiled and said, "Yeah, man—you better sell that plane. It's never gonna' be the same after three hours of our smelly asses."

The jokes continued for another few minutes and the bus whizzed down the private road back to main building. Murphy looked at Mackey with a pained expression.

Mackey looked at him quizzically. "What is it, Dex?"

"You guys really do *stink*!" he said with a fake smile.

"Let's see what you smell like after a few days in the fucking swamp. *Sir*."

"No offense, senior chief," said Dex.

"Chief petty officer, actually," said Cascaes.

Dex smiled and stood up. He reached into his jacket and pulled out a collar pin of a silver anchor with a star above it. "Excuse me, everyone," he said at the top of his lungs. The team went silent and looked at Dex, who stood up on the moving bus and held up the insignia of a Senior chief petty officer. "CPO Cascaes had been promoted as a result of his actions leading his team against enemy forces last year. You will now address him as Senior Chief Petty Officer Cascaes."

The entire bus erupted into applause and few "ooras." Dex signaled for quiet. "Wait—there's more. In recognition of exceptionally meritorious service to the government of the United States of America in a duty of great responsibility, Senior Chief Petty Officer Christopher Cascaes is hereby awarded the Navy Distinguished Service Medal."

Dex pulled a box from his jacket and opened it to reveal the medal as well as the ribbon—navy blue with a stripe of gold. "Congratulations, senior chief." He handed the box to Chris, who was dumbfounded.

"Thank you, sir, but it's my crew that deserves the recognition."

Dex smacked his shoulder. "From what I hear, your crew will be receiving the Presidential Unit Citation. Congratulations, men."

The SEALs, who had all worked together for many years, hugged and high-fived each other, then sat quietly, feeling embarrassed in front of the others, who hadn't been on that last fateful mission that prevented a nuclear holocaust.

Mackey shook hands with Cascaes, who sat looking at the new insignia in his palm.

"Too bad you won't be wearing your uniform for a while," said Mackey. "You deserve it, Chris. I'll go to war with you any day."

Chris finished the hand shake and said, "Good—because I think you are about to."

CHAPTER 17

Langley

The team had arrived in time for showers, a change of clothes, and dinner. As soon as they had been well fed, they returned to the tiny auditorium which served as their briefing room. They were seated when Leah and her assistant walked in after Darren and Dex. Even though at forty-four she was old enough to be the mother of a couple of the men, she still brought a few very quiet comments. The men hadn't been around women since Hawaii, and even a "well-preserved fossil", as Santos called her, was eye candy.

Darren Davis was the first to address the room from the lectern up front. He pressed a few buttons and a satellite image of the tri-border region appeared, with an overlay of country borders and blue lines to highlight water features.

"Good evening, gentlemen. Sorry to pull you out of the mosquito infested, alligator filled. nasty swamps of Florida. But there is some *good* news—you will be going to the mosquito infested, alligator filled, nasty swamps of Brazil and Paraguay. Allow me to introduce Latin-America Desk Chief Leah Pereira. She covers all of Central and South America, and this will be a joint operation between her and my personnel."

Leah stepped to the podium and smiled. "Good evening, everyone. This is my assistant desk chief, Connie Jones."

Santos quietly leaned over to Earl Jones, who was sitting next to him, and whispered, "Yo man, you didn't tell me yo' momma' worked here, too." Earl just gave him "the look."

Leah pressed a button and changed slides to show a half a dozen men. "Since 9-11, my department has been given greater authority in dealing with drugs and weapons smugglers. While in the past, this was strictly FBI, ATF, or DEA jurisdiction; the president recognized that drug and weapons dealings were typically connected with terrorist activity in this region. For the past eight years, we have been carefully monitoring activity between the Middle East and South and Central America. If you believe that only turban-wearing, Arab-sounding men want you dead, you would be incorrect."

She walked around the podium and pulled out a laser pointer to discuss the six men on the screen. She pointed to the first one, who was in fact wearing a turban.

"This beauty is Ali Aziz. He is about sixty and originally a Saudi. He *is* Arab and turban wearing and he *does* want you dead. He has lived in Beirut and moved around in Syria and the West bank. He is Al Qaeda. He is also a weapons smuggler and a killer of women and children. Everything from buses in Tel Aviv to the assassination of Ambassador McKnight a few days ago. While we can't prove the McKnight connection yet, we do know that he was in the region and was supposed to fly out of Paraguay to Syria, and we were prepared to pick him and these two up at the airport. They got spooked and never showed." She pointed at the next face, much younger and harder looking.

"This man is Hakim Bin-Salaam. He is known to move around with this man, Raman Qasim. Bin-Salaam and Qasim are professional killers. We have been close a few times to grabbing them, but they have lots of help in South America. We have lost two good agents in three years trying to take them down. Remember those faces. If they see you before you see them, they'll be the last faces you see. The list of their activities would fill ten folders, and of course we can't prove anything to the satisfaction of to the South American governments. They are more scared of reprisals for cooperating than of losing our aid on a national level. And of course, the terrorists pay better than we do when it comes to bank accounts in the Caymans."

She pointed to a grainy picture of a Latino man in Fidel Castro-looking fatigues. He even had the cigar in his mouth. "This is Enrique Antonio Vega. He is currently the largest exporter of raw cocaine in the tri-border area, and acts with total impunity. None of the three countries will admit he is operating inside their borders. Brazil tried to cooperate a few years back, and it led to assassinations of their best and brightest. They want nothing to do with us now. We are not sure how high his payments go in the governments of Paraguay, Argentina, and Brazil—but we work under the assumption that no one can be trusted down there who isn't one of us. And I mean no one."

She pointed to two terrible pictures of two other men.

"These two men are known associates of Vega and work directly for him. We believe one goes by the name Carlos. We have no other information on these two, but assume that they are his captains down there."

Leah turned off the projector and turned on the lights.

She paused and chose her words carefully. "Going into the jungle after Vega and these three terrorists will not be like anything you've done before. I know you are all highly trained professionals, but I have to ask—show of hands please, how many of you have ever been in the deep jungle before, not counting the Everglades trip?"

She was relieved when most of the hands went up.

"Well that's a pleasant surprise. Although I can tell you that the area where Vega is operating will be *much* tougher than Panama, El Salvador, or Southeast Asia. Tomorrow morning, I will have a specialist here to discuss the jungle with you. You may only remember ten percent of what he tells you, but maybe that will save your life. There are animals, plants and insects where you are going that are not like anything you've seen before. I'm afraid Vega may be the easy part." She paused. "Any of you know who the Guarani Indians are?"

Only Mackey and Cascaes had been briefed at all about them, the others sat expressionless.

"The Guarani Indians are the indigenous people of the area, like our own Native Americans. They were treated about as well, too. They were either enslaved or killed off by the Portuguese and Spaniards, who also shared their diseases with the Indians. Today's Guaranis live like most conquered peoples—in poverty and neglect, with high rates of unemployment, suicide and alcoholism. One of the tribes, the Pampidos Guarani, returned to the deep jungle over forty years ago. They have gone back to their old ways—*all* of them."

She paused and looked around the room. None of the men knew what she was hinting at.

"When Enrique Vega used his Guarani tribe as his personal army against the Cortez Cartel last year, his warriors not only killed everyone they saw—they ate most of them as well."

Earl Jones couldn't hold back his audible, "Holy shit!"

Eric Hodges, the marine sharpshooter quietly said, "You gotta' be shittin' me."

"I am not kidding you, gentlemen. These Guaranis are basically a Stone Age people living among AK-47-carrying drug dealers and international terrorists. And while they have no political agenda, they are not to be treated lightly. They use basic bows and arrows, poison blow darts and wooden clubs— and they are fearless. They are known as the "invisible people" because they can move through the jungle quickly and quietly. I am not telling you all of this to scare you, merely to put you on your toes. We tried once before to get out into the jungle to gather intelligence on Vega. The one who made it out needed counseling for a long time. The other two, well, you *don't* want to go out that way."

Leah walked over to a chair and sat, then looked at Darren, signaling she was done talking for a bit.

CHAPTER 18

Vega's Camp

Enrique didn't have to say much to convince the Chief once he showed him the rum. Rum had been a bone of contention between the two. The chief constantly demanded it for himself and his warriors, and Vega constantly made stories up about not having any, or it having gone bad, or whatever he could think of at the time to avoid giving it the chief. The Guaranis, like the American Indians, were *not* good drinkers. Those Guaranis that lived "civilized" usually ended up as alcoholic day laborers, the very reason the Pampidos had returned to the jungle a few generations before. Apparently, Kuka had forgotten about that.

Kuka grabbed the bottle and Vega showed six fingers. Kuka mumbled something so fast that Vega wasn't sure what to expect, but then the chief began pulling women out of the crowd that was celebrating and pushing them towards Vega. Vega then began handing them out to his men like beverages, keeping his favorite two for himself. One of them had known Vega from a month or so before, and was terrified when the chief grabbed her again.

While most people didn't know it, the Guaranis had actually invented the 'birth control pill'. They used plants that grew in the jungle to abort unwanted pregnancies, and had done so for hundreds of years. It had kept their bloodlines free from the white invaders, and made the business transactions less problematic between Vega and the chief.

The tribal medicine man, an ancient, ugly dog by the name of Manguk was constantly boiling *something*. Manguk supplied the poison for the darts, potions for remaining invisible in the jungle as well as the green paint, birth control potions, and hexes against enemies. He also oversaw executions of prisoners and the rights of cannibalism. It wasn't just a meal—it was an event. Manguk answered only to Kuka, whose word was absolute and unquestionable. As scared as the Guaranis were of old Manguk, Kuka was *still* 'the man.'

Vega took his two women by the wrists and escorted them roughly back to his cabin. His men each had their own way of dealing with their women. One had simply thrown a young girl over his shoulder, another had carried one under his arm like a briefcase, and the other two were simply walked back to the small huts of Vega's men. There were more men than women, the bottle of rum having netted only six girls, which meant taking turns and a long night for the unfortunate young captives. As pissed as Vega's men were for having to share women while Vega got *two*, they would never voice that, even to each other. Vega had once blown the head off of one of his men in front of the entire village and given the corpse to Manguk. The remaining men were "fiercely loyal" after that.

As usual, when Vega got back to his cabin, he pushed alcohol on the two young women to avoid them fighting back so hard. In his own mind, he was a porn star, and wished he could somehow convince the two young terrified girls that they were actually bisexual nymphomaniacs that just couldn't get enough of him and each other. It never turned out that way, though, and Vega typically ended up raping them one at a time over the course of the evening, while the other was tied and forced to watch. Even drunk, the Guarani women wanted nothing to do with him.

His men, currently numbering an even dozen, were all doing relatively the same things in their own smaller huts, although several of them were slightly rougher than even

Vega. For them, it had been many months since they had any kind of action at all with a woman, and had less respect for the Guarani women than even for the prostitutes they paid for in Paraguay or Brazil. Vega's men were drunk and loud, although not quite as loud as Kuka and his warriors.

Back near the large campfires, Kuka's warriors passed the rum and danced in a large circle around the campfire, waving spears and clubs and occasionally leaping over the fire. The women and children kept up their singing and dancing as well, as the jungle was turned into a scene from another world. As the sun began to set, shadows from the dancers around the fire leaped through the trees, making the jungle appear more haunted than usual. It wasn't long before Kuka decided he needed more rum, and he ran up to Vega's cabin.

Kuka walked through the curtain that was Vega's front door to find him behind a young woman on all fours, her face buried in her arm as she suffered quietly. The other woman was curled up in a ball in a corner naked, trying to recover from Vega's repeated rapes. The abrubicha demanded more rum, completely oblivious to Vega in the middle of his sexual escapades. Vega turned to face the chief, still on his knees gripping the young girl by the hips and told him to get the fuck out. That wasn't a good idea. Kuka, now drunk, kicked over Vega's desk and started screaming at Vega again for more rum. He walked over to the girl Vega was raping and pulled her up by her wrists, leaving Vega on his knees with his erection standing in the middle of nowhere. Now Vega wasn't happy either, and was equally drunk. He stood up, still erect, and began screaming back at Kuka, who pulled the girl away and pushed her out of the hut. She didn't need to be asked to start running away as fast as her legs would carry her.

Kuka was screaming now, pointing at the cabinet where Vega kept his bottles of rum. In his drunken rage, he was speaking fast and slurring, making it hard for Vega to understand exactly what he was saying. When he started pointing at the other girl, who was backed into the corner and tied by the wrist to a beam on the cabin wall, Vega relented. He walked over to the cabinet and took a key from a small crack behind the cabinet and unlocked the door. He took out a bottle, this one at full strength, and slowly handed it to the chief. In his broken Guarani, he asked the chief not to allow his men to get too wild, referring to the fighting that occurred last time. Kuka, already wild eyed, snatched the bottle, told Vega he could keep the girl as long as he wanted, and ran back to his little soirée by the fire.

Vega grabbed another bottle, this one for himself, and took a swig. He pointed it at the girl, asking her if she wanted some, but she merely crawled back further into the corner, trying to become invisible. Vega was standing there bare-ass naked when one of his men banged on the wall near the curtain doorway and yelled to his boss inside.

"Fuck," grumbled Vega. *"What is it?"* he yelled back.

"Sorry, boss, but I think you'd better come down to the ogas."

Vega cursed repeatedly and fumbled around until he found his underwear and camo pants. He walked out bare-chested, proud to display the claw marks on his arms and back.

"What now? I'm trying to get laid," he snapped at the man named Stefano.

"It's Eduardo, boss. He got drunk and didn't feel like waiting his turn to get laid, so he went down to the village to grab another girl. The Guaranis are all drunk and he started a fucking war down there. You better come quick, boss."

"Jesus Christ. I give you guys a fucking present and this is how you repay me? I *need* these fucking Indians, Stefano." Vega ran, without shoes or shirt towards the village, then stopped, spun around, and ran back to jam a .45 into his pocket. He and Stefano arrived at the center of the village, between the ogas where the fires were, in time to see Eduardo and two warriors screaming at each other nose to nose. Eduardo's nose wasn't the one with the large sharpened boar bone through it.

Vega walked into the center of the crowd, and the music stopped. Kuka appeared from the back of the crowd holding an almost empty bottle of rum. He was obviously hammered.

"Oh *great*," said Vega out loud when he saw the chief's condition. Vega's men slowly began to arrive, anxiously watching the scene unfold.

In his slurring drunken speech, Kuka told Vega, who understood the basic sentiment, that this pig Eduardo was trying to take another girl, and this girl was the warrior's daughter and not available for Eduardo's entertainment. On top of that, Vega's men had abused their privileges, since the other women had returned bruised and somewhat beaten. Furthermore, Kuka had only been paid for six, and now this man wanted a seventh. A seventh that he couldn't have had at any price, anyway. In the chief's mind, it was a big deal and he wanted retribution.

Vega tried to explain to the chief that he had given him that second bottle, so his man thought they could have more women. The chief had forgotten it was his second bottle, blasted as he was, and walked in circles for a moment while he pondered that. Vega was hoping that would end it, and it might have, had not the girl's father, one of Kuka's best warriors started screaming at Eduardo. Eduardo, drunk himself, and now getting scared, pushed the Guarani. Big mistake. The chief saw him push the warrior, something that was tantamount to an act of war. The Guaranis didn't "play fight." Kuka picked up a macanas by the fire. It was a long wooden club that had been inset with alligator teeth so it looked like a giant alligator jawbone. Kuka crossed the distance between him and Eduardo in an instant, leaping high through the air like a howler monkey while bringing the club down with both hands on Eduardo's face.

Vega screamed, "*No!*' but it was over in an instant. The cracking noise echoed through the jungle and Eduardo dropped like a rock, dead before he hit the ground, his face literally split in two. Vega's men ran towards Eduardo, but Vega stepped in front of them and held them back. The insulted warrior, father of the girl that Eduardo had tried to take home, knelt on Eduardo's chest and reached in to pull out Eduardo's warm brains. He pulled them out and showed them to Kuka, who grunted, allowing the drunken warrior to take a bite out of them before throwing them into the fire. That brought a cheer from the others, and sent chills down the spines of Vega and his men, who were now slowly backing away.

Vega spoke evenly to Kuka and said in Guarani, "This is over, chief. My men are going back to their huts. No more killing."

Kuka dismissed Vega but told Vega that Eduardo was now property of Manguk. Hearing the word Manguk, Vega's men got the gist and immediately began protesting to Vega, who told them to shut up.

"Unless we all want to end up like Eduardo, slowly back away and get back to my cabin. Get your AKs and ammo up. Slowly—now go."

Vega's men did what they were told, as they were outnumbered thirty to one and terrified as they watched Kuka's warriors begin shooting arrows into Eduardo's body as a final insult. Kuka's men did not consider Eduardo a warrior, but rather a piece of cheap meat. Eating him would not give them power, but soup was soup, so they would bring him to Manguk.

Vega and his men walked backwards, watching the drunken warriors beating and dismembering the bloody mess that had been one of their own a few moments before. As soon as they were thirty yards away, they sprinted back to their cabins to grab weapons and barricade themselves inside Vega's cabin. Vega threw the girl out to return to her family, lest that make things worse, and loaded weapons to prepare for a long night surrounded by drunken cannibals. Although the Guaranis rarely ventured outside their ogas past dark, Vega was taking no chances.

Down by the fires, the music began again, and the smell of meat cooking filled the jungle. Vega and his men remained holed up in Vega's hut, weapons ready, through the longest night of their lives. The sight and sound of Eduardo's head being opened and his brains being pulled out and eaten was something none of them would ever forget. The sweat that poured from their bodies wasn't just from the jungle heat—it was from stark terror.

CHAPTER 19

Langley

Darren Davis had spent the better part of three hours going over details of the team's cover story that they had worked out with Julia Ortiz. Leah's people had arranged for a Connex container full of building supplies and lumber that had already been brought to Langley. Once on site, it was unloaded to allow the weapons and gear to be stowed in the back of the container in crates marked as tools. Once that was loaded, the lumber and building materials were put back, completely obscuring the crates in the back. With the large quantity of materials, even if they were stopped and searched, no inspector would take out every single item to get to the hidden crates.

The team had enough food, ammunition and gear to operate for three weeks in the jungle if they had to, but they were trying for a week to ten-day mission, max. Unlike most missions, they couldn't pinpoint everything because the jungle terrain was extremely difficult, and the exact location of Vega's camp was unknown. A couple of the Guaranis that Julia helped at her outreach facility would act as guides, but even they hadn't traveled as far back into the jungle as Vega was reportedly located. The jungle was so thick that satellite imagery was useless, even at night. The campfires and other heat signatures were too weak to show up even to the most sensitive settings of their satellite computers. They'd have to do it the old fashioned way, using rafts and walking through unexplored jungle. For the SEALs and marines, it was a big change from normal operations, which were exact in planning and execution. For the rangers and CIA operatives that had worked with them in Afghanistan, it wasn't that far a stretch. Many of their missions in the mountains had been carried out without timetables and exact locations, relying on local populations for aid and intelligence.

The team did have jungle camouflage uniforms, but they were packed with the gear. For the purposes of traveling to Paraguay, they were given blue jeans, work boots and obnoxious yellow t-shirts that read "Outreach Ministries of Greater Los Angeles." There was a large cross with "Matthew 25" written below it, and in a circle around the cross it read: "Whatever you did for one of the least of these brothers of mine, you did for me."

Mackey read it and asked Cascaes, "If I am wearing this when I kill somebody, ya' think I'll go straight to Hell?"

Cascaes smiled and said, "Stay alive and you won't have to worry about it."

One of the SEALs, a quiet young Jewish kid named Jonathan Cohen smiled when he held up his shirt. "My grandmother is going to turn over in her grave," he said with a laugh.

Davis heard him and laughed. "Don't worry Jon—your new passport has you as Jon Murphy. Make sure you can spell it."

Davis got control back over the meeting after the men had a few minutes to throw their shirts on and start preaching to each other. He let them joke around and genuflect to each other, then clapped his hands twice, and everyone settled down.

"Mack," asked Davis, "You have a medic in this crew?"

Mack looked at Cascaes, who pointed to Ryan O'Conner and said, "O'Conner isn't an actual corpsman, but he has the most advanced first aid courses of my crew. What about you, lieutenant?" he asked Lt. Koches. "Didn't I see advanced first aid courses in your file?"

"Roger that, sir. rangers train like SEALs to be self-sufficient in the field. You wouldn't want me operating on you, but I can stitch and pop a chest tube."

"No thanks," replied Cascaes with a grin. "Stay the hell away from me unless I'm almost dead. Anybody else?"

The rest of the men had all been given first aid courses as part of their advanced combat training, but none of them were actual corpsmen.

Davis sat back and crossed his arms, frowning. "It's too late to shove somebody new into your group, but I have to tell you, I don't like you going out there without a doc. You can't call for a dust-off where you're going. Anybody gets hurt out there, they're walking out the same way you walked in. Could be a few days out. Mack?"

Mackey and Cascaes looked at each other and shrugged. Mackey asked, "I haven't had the luxury of a Medivac in twenty years. What do you think, Chris?"

Cascaes addressed Davis. "Sir, my team has always assumed we were on our own when we worked in the past. We've all been trained in basic first aid. Unless someone was very seriously injured, I think we're fine."

Leah had been listening and thinking while the men were speaking. She stood up. "Darren, I have an idea." Everyone turned to her, realizing now that when she had an idea, it was usually pretty good. "Down at the outreach facility, Julia has a doctor that gives immunizations and physicals and the usual kid stuff…"

Cascaes interjected. "With all due respect, ma'am, is this doc an old man? We are going to be going through some pretty rough jungle…"

"*She* is not old at all. Doctor Theresa Orlando is in her thirties. My guess is, it will be *you* trying to keep up with *her*. She has lived in Paraguay for two years now, helping Julia, and she works for us. She speaks some of the Guarani language and just might come in handy. Of course, that's assuming she'll go along with you into the unexplored jungle."

Mackey and Cascaes looked at each other and grimaced. Cascaes spoke, "Ma'am, I don't know. This will be a dangerous job. She has no combat experience…"

"Actually, she does. United States Navy corpsman. She was in Desert Storm One attached to the First Marines as a combat medic. I believe her Bronze Star is as shiny as yours, senior chief." She smiled and Cascaes was aware that she knew his file inside out, including the two Bronze Stars, a Purple Heart and his shiny new Navy Cross.

"I guess we'll meet the ladies in Paraguay," said Mackey.

"Guess so," said Cascaes quietly.

"'Bout time we had some chicks in this outfit anyway," said Ernie P. with a smile. "I was starting to worry about you guys…"

"Don't worry," said Moose from the row behind him, "You ain't my type."

Darren Davis stood up. "Okay, then that's it. Your gear is being assembled and transferred to airfreight as we speak and will be sent to a cargo ship in Puerto Rico. You will fly out the day after tomorrow, and will spend tomorrow working with our jungle warfare specialist doing more plant, insect and animal identifications. The guy is good—so pay attention to him. Tomorrow night we will go over your route again. You'll use the river as much as possible at night to move quickly. During the day, you'll disappear in the jungle. The Paraguayan government doesn't know you are coming, and you'll be uninvited guests. Stick to your cover story and stay out of sight once you leave Julia's clinic. You men are going back in time a few hundred years, and this won't be like anything you've done before, so stay sharp and look out for each other.

We still haven't been able to confirm the whereabouts of Qasim, Aziz or Bin-Salaam, but will be working on the assumption that they are still around. Hopefully, you'll take out the whole bunch of them, but even if you only get Vega and take out his operation; it will be considered a success. The director really wants those three scumbags, though— McKnight was a personal friend of his. If we are able to get any decent intelligence on them, it will be forwarded to you while you are in the field. Any questions for now?"

Cascaes answered, "Sir? What about the Guaranis? Are these tribal people considered hostile combatants? What are the rules of engagement with them?"

Davis looked over at Leah and raised his eyebrows. It wasn't his call.

Leah exhaled thoughtfully and crossed her arms, looking at her shoes for a moment. Finally, she looked up and grimaced. "Look, these people are being *used* by Vega. They have no point of reference as to what he's doing out there. If possible, I'd prefer to leave them out of this. That said, Vega used them in the past as his personal army against other drug lords, and I think you know that they ate his biggest competitors. If you are attacked, you're free to respond. We'd like Vega and his men removed permanently. As far as the Guaranis go—if they take off into the jungle, you have no reason to pursue them." She was finished, but then added, "But do not take these people lightly. They use primitive weapons, but the blow darts are poisonous and deadly, and these warriors have no fear. The Guaranis that Julia works with are scared to death of those people, and these are people that know the jungle. I suggest you listen and learn from the locals, and steer clear of the Pampidos if possible."

"But we are cleared to fire?" asked Cascaes, wanting total clarity.

"Yes, if you feel that you are in danger, you're cleared to fire." It bothered Leah to say that, but she also knew that these were fierce cannibals, and being used or not, they were extremely dangerous.

The men were dismissed and assembled outside to work out and run. They would push themselves hard, as usual, to prepare physically and mentally for what would surely be a rough trip.

CHAPTER 20

Vega's Camp

Vega and his men spent the entire night awake and on guard. His cabin was up a small trail away from the center of Kuka's tribal camp, where the ogas were located in a clearing around the central fire pits. The long houses were home to almost three hundred Guarani men, women and children. Vega and his men sat facing out of every direction of the hut, waiting for an attack that never came. The men were thoroughly freaked out, after having seen one of their own killed so violently, and then watching his brains being eaten by a man that could only be described as a savage. No one spoke much during the night, even as they smelled their friend being roasted while the drums and singing grew louder all night long.

Fortunately, after the warriors had feasted and gotten drunk, they returned to their ogas to celebrate inside, where most of them passed out from the alcohol. By the time the sun came up and the sounds of the jungle grew loud again with the screeching of birds and buzzing of insects, the entire Guarani tribe was sleeping.

Vega and his men looked like hell. Most of them hadn't slept more than an hour or two, in shifts, and they were nursing their own hangovers and graphic images that were permanently burned into their brains. They would think twice before looking at the Guarani women again.

Carlos was the first to speak as they stood up and stepped out into the sunshine, their AK-47s loaded and at the ready. "What are we going to do, boss?"

Vega looked harshly at Carlos and his men. "Nothing! We are going to do nothing! If the chief wanted us dead last night, we'd all be roasting over his fire. I will find a new hiding spot for the rum while they are asleep and if he asks, I'll tell him it's gone. Eduardo got himself killed—it's not my fault. I suggest you keep alert and stay together in groups of three or more for the next couple of hours until we see how Kuka is feeling when he wakes up. I don't want this incident screwing up my production. In two years, we're all rich and out of this God forsaken jungle. Don't mess this up or I'll kill you myself."

Vega's men left his cabin like scolded schoolchildren and returned to their own huts in search of potable water and aspirin. Carlos and another man stayed with Vega as bodyguards. They sat out on his little porch and ate a few bananas with rice as they waited for Kuka to wake up.

The sound of Vega's radio squelching was a big surprise. Carlos walked over and retrieved it for Vega, who said a quiet "Who is this?"

"Señor Vega, it is Hakim. We're getting close to your camp again, but will need a few of your Indians (as he always called them) to bring us in before we get totally lost."

"Hakim? What are you doing here? I thought you were long gone, back across the Atlantic Ocean again?" asked a surprised Vega.

"Problems at the airports. It appears that we are wanted men for the time being. We need to disappear for a while. Your camp is ideal. We're at the river. We got a ride back down from our Iranian friends, but we need you to bring us back. How long will it take?"

Vega took his finger off the transmitter and asked Carlos, "Can you find a couple of sober Guaranis and get back to the river?"

Carlos nodded.

"Tomorrow afternoon. All three of you are there?"

"Yes. We will look for you tomorrow afternoon. Out."

Vega sat back and wiped his tired face with a bandana and said, "Well at least the Guaranis will have more to eat if this goes south."

CHAPTER 21

Santos Airport, Brazil

The team landed in Santos in the morning, after an overnight commercial flight out of Dulles. They landed wearing sandals or sneakers, cargo shorts and their yellow T-Shirts. If they looked goofy, no one was going to say it to their faces. They were fairly nervous going through immigration and customs in Santos since it was their first time ever using false ID's, with the exception of Mackey and the other three CIA agents, who used them all the time. They cruised through without a hitch, and even had a few people "bless them and their good work" in the airport

They left through customs and picked up their luggage of civilian clothes to jibe with their cover story and then headed out to pick up a shuttle to the rent-a-car place at the other end of the airport. There, they picked up two white Mitsubishi "cab-over" vans, similar to Volkswagen beetle vans that Mackey remembered from his youth. They drove through the highly industrial area to the center of town, where they checked into a small hotel that was expecting them. Julia wouldn't be in Santos until the next day, when the container ship was due to arrive at the port.

The men checked in, threw their luggage into their rooms, and did what guys always do in a new city—they walked until they found a place to eat and drink and look at women. They had changed out of their T-shirts, thrown on jeans and casual clothes, and found a little café with seating outside that overlooked a shopping area. With an entire day to kill, and a "company American Express Card," they would enjoy the day.

The waitress didn't speak much English or Spanish, but Cascaes surprised everyone with a little Portuguese. He ordered Caipirinhas and beers for everyone, with some Feijoada (black beans) and Churrasco.

"Where the hell did you learn to speak Portuguese?" asked Mackey after the cute little waitress left, not oblivious to the stares and comments the men made about her. They had practically taken over the entire outside seating area.

"*Cascaes!*" he replied, "It's a Portuguese name," He laughed. "I'm first generation American, Chris. My parents both spoke fluent Portuguese. I'm not fluent anymore, but I know enough to get us food and beers."

"Yo' skipper, what did you order? I don't want no Taco Bell," said Earl with a smile.

"Don't worry, it's barbeque—you'll dig it. But watch the Caipirinhas—drink too many and *you'll* be speaking Portuguese, too."

"Yeah, man—what is that stuff?" asked Earl.

"Cachaca and lime. Similar to turpentine or butane," he said with a smile.

"Oh, great" said Moose, "get everyone hammered and then go out working…"

Mackey shot him a look—there was to be no referring to working at all in public.

"You know," said Moose, "Saving the souls of our brothers with a hangover." He smiled.

Raul Santos stood up and opened his arms wide. "Welcome to my city, my friends—Santos, Brazil, named after the famous American explorer who discovered beer." Everyone laughed and thanked him for allowing them to drink beer in his city.

The banter continued until the waitress returned with a busboy and trays of food. It was enough to feed an army, which by coincidence was exactly what they needed. To be able to

relax like gentlemen on a beautiful sunny day overlooking
little shops and the ocean was a treat that most of them hadn't
enjoyed before during a mission. At one point during the meal,
Mackey looked around at the men and realized no one had
spoken in almost five minutes. Each man was staring at the
sea, sipping cold drinks and enjoying his full belly. It was a
perfect moment, and Mackey smiled ear to ear.

Cascaes caught him smiling and looked back at the men.
For a second, he felt a little choked up, feeling the love and
pride he had for this crew, especially his SEALs. They had
all saved each other's ass more times than they could count,
and now, to sit totally relaxed overlooking the ocean that was
a sailor's home as they prepared for the unknown yet again
was just a beautiful place to be. Cascaes gave Mackey's fist a
pound with his own fist, and they didn't have to say a word to
know what the other felt.

Cascaes ordered a couple of orders of flan for dessert, just so
the guys could try something new. The sweet custard brought
mixed reviews, but the Caipirinhas had been a hit, and the men
were a little buzzed. Mackey paid the bill and the men spent
the rest of the day walking around the city like regular tourists.
They wanted to enjoy every minute of the Brazilian sunshine,
and so they walked to the beach.

Only Mackey and Cascaes were prepared for the Brazilian
beach scene. Men and women in Brazil didn't sunbath like
Americans. The women, most of whom were topless, wore
thongs that weren't much wider than dental floss as bottoms,
and the men's suits weren't much bigger. Mackey laughed and
commented it was the first time he'd seen his crew speechless.
The men sat up on the boardwalk drinking cold beer and
staring shamelessly for hours. It was a *good day*.

CHAPTER 22

Vega's Camp

Vega sat on the ground in front of his cabin facing Kuka. Carlos sat back on the porch about thirty feet away, AK-47 across his lap, watching intently. Two of Kuka's warriors sat on their haunches down the trail a bit. Obviously, both "chiefs" were a little tense about the meeting. Although Vega spoke some of the Guarani language, the subtleties needed in a complicated conversation were lacking, and it was frustrating for Vega to try and express himself in what amounted to third grade thoughts.

Over the course of fifteen minutes, Vega was able to convey that eating Eduardo was not acceptable behavior to Vega. Kuka, for his part, was fairly blasé about the whole incident. As far as he was concerned, Eduardo had insulted one of his best warriors, and Vega and his men had been too rough with their women. Kuka hinted that any future contact with his women would be very costly, if he was to allow it to happen again. Vega told Kuka that he needed the women to get busy again harvesting the Coca leaves, and explained that they needed much more than they had been producing. Kuka was fine with that, as long as he would be compensated. Rainey season was coming soon, and tarps and blankets would be required in larger quantities. Kuka had been given an umbrella once by Vega, which he had in turn given to one of his wives. The umbrella was very impressive to the whole tribe, and now Kuka wanted two more. It was hard for Vega not to smile at the hard bargain Kuka was demanding for millions of dollars worth of cocaine.

In the end, Vega promised Kuka umbrellas, steel pots, knives, tarps and blankets and some jewelry for the women. In return, Kuka promised his men wouldn't harm Vega's men again so long as they behaved themselves, and Kuka would make sure the women got busy finding and drying the leaves. Kuka's hangover was sufficient enough that he never mentioned rum. Vega lit a cigar and let Kuka puff on it a few times, but Kuka hacked his brains out and gave it back to Vega. He left smiling, and all was well in the jungle kingdom again, just in time for the arrival of Vega's Middle Eastern houseguests.

Vega's men were still a little uneasy around the Guaranis, and remained armed and in small groups. The Guaranis didn't hold a grudge, and acted as if the whole incident had never occurred. Justice had been done, and the event was finished. The fact that Eduardo's smashed skull had been boiled out and was hanging somewhere in Manguk's hut was not lost on Vega's men, however, and the once relaxed atmosphere was still very tense to the outnumbered foreigners.

By the time the sun was getting ready to drop behind the top of the forest canopy, two Guaranis entered the camp leading three tired looking Arabs. They had called in a few times over the past few hours, and Vega had instructed his men to cook up some fish for his weary guests. The tension wasn't lost on the three outsiders when they entered the camp. They greeted Enrique and immediately asked if there was something going on, as they were nervous enough about their own problems with the authorities. Vega related the incident, which made the three men obviously uncomfortable, but they didn't say much about it other than the fact they were happy it was over and Kuka had control over his people again.

"How long will you stay?" asked Vega.

Hakim smiled. "Did you know, in my country, it is considered rude to ask a guest how long they will stay with you? Are we unwanted in your camp, Señor Vega?"

Vega smiled and made light of it. "Of course not!" he said with a big smile. "In fact, I am happy to have three more 'civilized men' to add to our numbers. You are perfectly safe from the police here, and I am reasonably sure you are safe from the Guaranis now, as well. I will have to send my men out in the next few days though to pick up some supplies to keep the crazy old chief calm, though. For a few minor supplies, I can keep my little army producing and under control. Can I get anything for you when they go to the city?"

"Perhaps some mosquito repellent, if you would be so kind," said Raman Qasim. "I don't know how you get used to this jungle. It is amazing you don't all have malaria."

"Who said we don't?" said Vega, half serious. "And God knows what else. I won't be unhappy to leave this place one day soon. In any event, I have a few cans in my cabin. You may help yourself. There are nets to sleep in as well."

Qasim bowed slightly and said thank you, then added, "Your men did very well last week, Señor Vega. While it made our departure too risky, I do have to tell you that the worldwide reaction was even more than we could have expected. The American stock market fell another five hundred points, flights were cancelled, and everyone is screaming at each other on the television. America grows weaker by the day."

Vega tried a polite smile, but inside was concerned about losing his best customers. He changed the subject. "Come, you must be tired. My men have prepared a feast. Carlos! Take care of our guests!" He clapped his hands, and his men came jogging over to escort the men to a large fire where two five foot catfish were roasting. Dinner would be fresh and delicious, and much less controversial than the night before's.

CHAPTER 23

Santos, Brazil

The two Chrises were sitting outside at a little café enjoying Brazilian coffee and a sweet roll, waiting for Mackey's cell phone to ring with a call from Julia. The rest of the team had slept in a bit, after consuming a few extra beers the night before.

Mackey put his coffee down and leaned closer to Cascaes. "Ya' know, when I live like an actual *human being*, like on a beautiful morning like this, I realize how many of my years have been spent living like a fucking animal. I think this is my last gig, Chris. You know I always say I'm too old for this shit…well, I'm getting too old for this shit. My buddy Skripak was right—it's time to get out while I can still walk."

"Yeah? Then what? You don't strike me as the type to sit around doing nothing," said Cascaes.

"I didn't say doing *nothing*. I can fly commercial—or maybe just see the world as a civilian for a while, instead of always attacking it. There's a difference."

Cascaes laughed. "Yeah, well, with my promotion, I think I'll stick around for a while. Besides, I love what I do, and these guys are my family…"

Mackey's cell phone rang. He picked up and said hello, and a very sweet voice with a British accent said "hello" back.

"Señor Mackey, from the Los Angeles Outreach Ministry, I presume? It's Julia."

Mackey was still trying to get over the British accent. "Julia, nice of you to call. I'm just having a coffee and enjoying a beautiful morning. Care to join us?"

"Sounds lovely, darling, but I'm down at the dock presently, waiting for your Connex container."

Mackey put his hand over the mouthpiece and whispered to Cascaes, *"She called me darling..."*

"Well, shall we meet you down there?" he asked.

"No, actually, it's probably better if I go it with my usual people. I will give you a ring when we have the truck loaded and ready to go. We'll swing by your hotel and you can follow us out. Have your men ready, by say, ten o'clock?"

"You have a date," he said, already meaning it like a *real* date just from the sound of her voice. He looked at Mackey, "A British accent. That kills me, man. I thought for sure she would sound Spanish or something."

Cascaes just laughed.

"We'll finish our coffee and wake up the crew and get them fed. She's coming by at ten, and it's going to be a long trip."

The two of them finished the coffees, the best they had ever had, and took the long way back to the hotel so they could see the beach again. The water was blue and clean—a far cry from the swamp they had just left, and the one they would soon enter. The team was assembled fairly quickly and had loaded up their vans just as another small van followed by a large tractor-trailer pulled up in front of the hotel. The van pulled over, and out of the passenger side door emerged a stunning young woman who stopped the entire team in their tracks.

Julia Ortiz had a bouncy walk that just read as "happy." Even though she was petit at five feet tall and a hundred pounds soaking wet, she was always the center of attention. She was wearing jeans and work boots with an old sweatshirt that had the sleeves cut off, and could not possibly have looked sexier if she had been wearing an evening gown. Her short black hair fluttered in the warm breeze and her teeth were ivory white against her tan skin. Even Cascaes, who tended to be "cooler" than the others said "holy shit" quietly to Mackey, who had instantly fallen in love.

Mackey strode out to greet the peppy young woman who approached the group with such confidence. He extended his hand and said, "You must be Julia Ortiz?"

She shook it with a firm handshake and said, "And you must be Señor Christopher?"

Her accent was rather bizarre. She looked as Brazilian as anyone walking in the city, but her accent was mostly British with only a little twang of something else—Portuguese or Spanish?

"That's me," Mackey smiled, "But most of my friends just call me Mack. This here is Chris Jensen, my assistant in our outreach program, and I'll introduce you to the rest of the fellas later, when their tongues are back in their mouths."

She shook hands with Cascaes, now using his fake passport name of Jensen. All of the military personnel in the group had been given new last names only. The CIA members had changed names so many times prior to this mission that it was safe to keep theirs' as they were. Dex Murphy had feared that if things got too complicated, one of the men might slip up, as they were not well trained in spy-craft. Since the major risk was with military records popping up on someone's computer somewhere, it was only *those* members of the team whose records were altered.

Julia ignored Mackey and disappeared into the group of men, introducing herself to each. Moose, who tended to be a large teddy bear when not killing people, gave her a hug and lifted her right off her feet. Not to be outdone, each team member after Moose gave her a kiss hello and his most charming smile. She was used to the attention, and played up to each of them. In only a few seconds, she had her own fan club.

She walked back to Mackey smiling, and said, "There, now we're old friends. Do you wish to travel with me in my van? We have a very long day of driving. It would give us an opportunity to chat a while."

"Sounds perfect," said Mackey. "Chris, you come with us. Will he fit?" he asked after he invited Chris.

"Yes, actually, I will have my two men drive your two vans, and I will drive you myself in this one." With that settled, her two helpers, hired by her in Paraguay three years ago, were introduced and headed out to drive the men across Brazil.

$$\oplus$$

The drive out of the city was slightly harrowing, with traffic coming from every direction, and no shortage of horn usage or cursing between drivers. Julia had commented that only drivers in New York or Rome were more insane. The small convoy of three vans and the truck managed to stay together and get to the highway out of the city that headed south-southwest towards Curitiba, one of the larger cities around the area. There, they would pick up the Rodovia Panamericana highway and head west towards Cascavel and to Foz do Iguacu, on the Paraguayan border.

Julia drove like a New Yorker, honking and cursing while smiling all the while, and chatting with the two Chrises. She commented that it was very polite to give them both the same name so she wouldn't forget. She asked why the rest of the team wasn't given the name Chris as well, and the two men couldn't help but instantly love her warmth and sense of humor.

"Are you *sure* you are CIA?" asked Mackey finally. "You are *way* too cute."

"CIA?" she asked with feigned shock. "Oh my! You mean, as in a *secret agent* or *spy* or something? How exciting! No, I just help the local Guaranis. But if I *was* CIA, it would be a much better cover than a platoon of commandos wearing Jesus Loves You T-shirts."

They all laughed. Finally, Julia smiled and spoke with a more serious voice. "I have been doing some poking around and it looks like your three targets have disappeared back into the jungle, I assume to Vega's camp. We had coordinated picking them up at several airports that we had leads on, but they must have gotten spooked."

"How much do you know about Vega and the three stooges?" asked Mackey, sitting in the middle of the front bench seat between Julia and Cascaes. Cascaes kept track of their friends via the side-mirror to make sure they stayed together.

"In Eastern Paraguay, Enrique Vega might as well be the president. He uses the Pampidos Guaranis as his own army, along with his own crew, the size of which is unknown. He is so deep in the jungle, we can't even get satellite images of anything that resembles a camp. We *do* know that he has wiped out every other coke smuggler in Eastern Paraguay, and whacked politicians in Paraguay, Brazil, and Argentina over the past six years. Everyone in the tri-border region is scared to death of him, and rightfully so. You saw what happened to McKnight. While Al Qaeda in Iraq may be claiming responsibility, I am damn sure it was Vega's people. So is the director, which is why you are here."

"So how is it you know so much about him, but no one knows where he is?" asked Mackey.

"The guy's like Bin Laden—he causes death and destruction but you never actually see him. He uses the Guaranis to transport his coke, which I know from my own Guaranis at the clinic. My Guaranis are terrified of Vega's tribe.

"The families I work with are just regular folks now, really. Poor Indians like the ones in the US on reservations—but Vega's tribe, they returned to the wild forty or fifty years ago and they are as savage now as they were two thousand years ago. I'm sure their family structures are similar to the Guaranis that I know, but they are still dangerous in the jungle. They killed and ate one of the Cartels that was competing against Vega—and *that's* a story I've heard enough times to believe."

"Yeah, so we were told," said Cascaes.

"Don't underestimate them," said Julia.

"We were told that, too," said Cascaes.

The three of them drove all day, stopping only once for fuel and a latrine break. By late afternoon they reached Foz do Iguacu on the Brazil-Paraguay border. The world's largest hydroelectric dam, the Itaipu Dam, was located near the falls, and the Iguassu Falls themselves were as large as three Niagara Falls. Julia stopped to get gas and all of the men got out to admire the view. It had to be one of the most amazing places any of them had ever seen.

Cascaes was standing next to Moose and Ripper, who were arguing about whether or not they could survive the fall into the water hundreds of feet below. Of course they both knew they'd be dead after hitting water that would seem like concrete, but neither of them would admit it.

Cascaes looked at his men and said, "Take a long look guys. It's really pretty from up here, but I have a feeling we are about to enter the *Twilight Zone* real soon. We need to cross the border without incident, so remind the guys to stay loose. Once we go over the damn, we're in Paraguay and Ciudad Del Este is right down the road. Once we go beyond that, it's the wild west."

"Good," said Moose, flatly. "We were all gonna' get fat and lazy if we did any more sitting around anyway. I'm ready to go play in the woods."

Cascaes laughed, knowing he meant it.

Mackey called out to his men, "Mount up, boys—time we get this show on the road."

They had refueled and got into the line of traffic headed over the damn to Paraguay. The check point on the Paraguay side was fairly lax, with border police giving cursory looks at the tourist's driver's licenses and passports. Julia had made the trip so many times and was so pretty that almost all of the guards knew her face. They called her the Guardian of the Guaranis, just like the local folks where she lived, and smiled and waved her through. She leaned out of the window and spoke to one of the guards she recognized, telling him that the vans and truck behind her were all with her, bringing supplies to build a school. He smiled and waved them all through, and the convoy headed into Paraguay.

"That is *so* not fair," said Mackey with a grin for his good-looking driver. "If that was me and Cascaes crossing without you, we'd be strip-searched by now."

"I'm surprised they didn't strip-search Julia," said Cascaes quietly, the closest thing to flirting he had done since meeting her.

"Well maybe next time you'll get lucky and a female border guard will strip-search both of you," said Julia.

"My luck, it will be a dude named Bubba," said Cascaes.

The decent highways of Brazil quickly went to hell as they proceeded west towards Ciudad del Este.

CHAPTER 24

Outside Ciudad Del Este

The convoy of vans and the tractor-trailer arrived at Julia's makeshift relief station in the late afternoon. A small sign read "International Center for Domestic Relief," but the sign was much fancier than the outpost. A wooden floor with poles holding up a thatched roof made up the largest building in the small camp. They were outside of the city, where Julia's "real office" was located, but this was where she spent most of her time. The camp was on the fringe of the jungle, where the Guaranis lived and worked. Julia and her helpers administered vaccines, taught Spanish and even some English, provided clothing and basic provisions and did what they could to improve the lives of the forgotten Indians. The Guaranis loved Julia, the children especially, and when the trucks arrived, the women and children began flowing out of the jungle and small buildings, instantly singing and smiling.

Julia hopped out of the van and was mobbed, as usual, by her young fans. She picked up a little boy of maybe five years old and gave him a hug. He was speaking fast in his native language, and although Mackey and Cascaes had no idea what he was saying, it was obvious that the boy loved Julia. A hug is a hug in any language. The rest of the men piled out of the vans and walked over towards their boss, but were immediately swallowed up by crowds of children who took them by their hands and started singing again. The high-pitched young voices filled the camp with a happy choir of unknown lyrics, and every man in the team was overcome.

Moose, the biggest of the bunch, had tears running down his face as a little girl literally climbed up his arm like he was a tree. She sat on his shoulder, laughing, and kissed him on top of his head, which was almost as big as her. He was the largest human she had ever seen, and for whatever reason, instantly adopted him. The others were equally taken in by the children, most of them wearing only loin cloths or ratty shorts. They were barefooted and without shirts, and they all were small and brown. The boys had bowl-cut shiny black hair; while the girls wore theirs in long pony tails. They were all smiling and genuinely happy to see visitors.

Julia clapped her hands a few times, and the children gathered around her and went quiet. She explained, in Spanish, that these visitors were here to build them a school, and she wasn't finished with the sentence when the cheering started. They all started singing again and made a huge circle, holding hands, while they danced around the men in the silly t-shirts.

"What the hell did she say?" asked Cascaes. "Think they are getting ready to eat us?"

Julia heard him and laughed. "*My* Guaranis are not cannibals, sir. I told them you were here to build them a school. And you *will*."

"Yes, ma'am," was all he could think of as he watched the smiling children sing and dance around his knees. The happy faces that surrounded them were contagious.

Another woman appeared from one of the small huts. She was in khaki fatigue pants and a tank top with a yellow smiley face on it. She waved and smiled as she approached Julia and the team.

"Gentlemen, say hello to Theresa Orlando. She's the closest thing to a doctor my Guaranis have ever seen."

Theresa was in her late thirties, and although attractive in a natural sort of way, she didn't hold a candle to Julia. She walked more like a guy, and had a marine's handshake. As Cascaes said hello, he though she reminded him of a girl that grew up with lots of older brothers.

"So you're all here from Los Angeles, huh?" asked Theresa. She had worked with Julia on and off for two years, through CIA, and had used her position as "local doctor" to get in and out of lots of out of the way places. She liked her work helping the locals as much as the intelligence aspect of it, and she and Julia were a perfect team.

Mackey smiled. "Yes, ma'am, praise the Lord."

Cascaes added an "Amen."

"Do me a favor and don't try and pass as missionaries around me. You suck as secret agents," said Theresa with a smile.

Mackey and Cascaes looked at each other, then at Julia, and then they all started laughing.

"Be nice to them, Theresa. They're going to build us our school," said Julia with her flirting smile. She looked at Mackey, who melted, and Julia added, "No school—no jungle tour."

"Just tell us where you want it," he said, totally under her spell.

"Well, maybe I'll let you all unpack and feed you first. The children have waited this long, you can start working tomorrow."

Cascaes smacked Mackey and motioned for him to look over at the men. Most of them were sitting on the ground, playing with children whose language they couldn't speak, but communicating just the same. Moose had three tiny kids on his shoulders, and more were trying to climb up his arms and legs. His grin was unprecedented.

"Bunch of trained killers?" said Mackey with a laugh.

Julia smiled at the scene of the hardened warriors being totally ruled by the children. "Careful," she said, "or you'll end up staying here."

Mackey looked at her beautiful face and smiled. "It wouldn't be the worst thing I ever did."

CHAPTER 25

Camp Hope

It was Cascaes who came up with the name while looking at his men.

"Camp Hope," he had said out loud. Mackey heard him and immediately knew what he was thinking. They instantly decided it was the perfect name for this little outpost of hope in the middle of nowhere. It had a strange effect on the men, and was especially healing for Earl Jones, who still had occasional dreams about the two dead children in Saudi. Although he had apologized to them in his dreams, and was doing much better, he still had days of feeling outright depressed. Now, surrounded by children, he was reborn. His smile had returned, like those of his comrades, and the general dynamic of the group had totally changed.

Gone were the macho barbs and typical military machismo. Instead, the men matured into instant "dads" to the hundreds of small children that flowed in and out of the camp. The first morning in camp, after arriving the night before and having a humble meal of rice and beans and some type of meat that no one asked about, the men immediately sprang into action unloading the building supplies. While none of them were construction workers, they were a team that knew how to work quickly and efficiently together. They unloaded beams, trusses, planks, bags of screws and nails, and boxes of tools happily, as the smiling children looked on, occasionally clapping their hands when something even mildly interesting happened—

like when Moose and Ripper carried a very large load of wood with two children sitting on it.

Julia and Theresa had told the men where they wanted the building, and the plans for construction had been drawn up and included with the shipment of lumber. Julia had personally overseen the building of the few huts and quasi-buildings in her camp, and knew her way around a hammer. With all of them working together, it was like an Amish barn raising, and the structure was completely finished by the afternoon of the second day. Cascaes had commented that all was missing was the school bell—a comment not missed by Julia, and after she spoke with some children, they returned with a large drum, which she presented to Chris.

"Your school bell, sir. Would you like to ring it?"

Cascaes laughed and banged on the drum a few times, and was amazed to see the Guaranis flowing out of the jungle into camp. "Wow," he said with a laugh. "This works better than revile!"

The Guaranis, men, women, and children, gathered around the new building that would serve as a school. They brought paints and feathers and pebbles and various sorts of primitive objects with which to decorate the walls, and Mackey's men were as enthusiastic about playing with the paints as the children were.

Cascaes was sitting on the new wooden floor watching some women painting when Julia sat next to him.

"You're second in command after Mackey?" she asked.

"I could tell you, but I'd have to kill you," he said with a smile.

"You *wouldn't*," she said in her sexiest voice, and he felt it in his chest.

"You're right. But I bet you kill every man you meet." He let that hang and she didn't respond. "I am second in command, yes. Why?"

"No reason, really. I just see the way the men look to you for instructions all the time, even when you aren't doing anything. I'm a people watcher, I guess. Makes me a good agent," she said.

"I see. And how the hell did *you* end up here? I'm not being rude, and I know you hear it all the time, but God, you're gorgeous. How did you end up in the Paraguayan jungle?"

She smiled without breaking eye contact. And yes, she did hear it all the time. "My father was in the shipping business. I lived in Singapore and Hong Kong for a few years as a very young girl. I don't remember too much of it, though, really. My mom died when I was only nine, in a car accident in Hong Kong. We returned to England after that."

"Sorry to hear about that," said Cascaes.

"Yes, well, that's life I suppose. It makes me sad that I don't remember more about her. Anyway, my father took a job in America the following year and off we went to San Francisco. He met another woman and remarried, and she became my second Mom. I have a half sister, too. Beth. She lives in Virginia."

"She gorgeous, too?" asked Chris.

"Way better looking, in fact. But she has four children and a husband, so you might not be as inclined to ask her out."

"As inclined as I am to ask you, you mean?" He could feel his face get red.

"Yes, right. We could go out to a movie, maybe dinner and dancing." She stood up and extended her hand to help him up. "Besides, you've got some work to do I believe."

She pulled him up and he stood, very close to her face. She was not one to be intimidated, and they just stood there for a minute.

"Thanks for building my school," she said, and kissed him quickly on his cheek.

She started to walk away, but he still had her hand. "Hey," was all he could muster.

She turned back around to face him, and smiled when she saw how red his face was. "Why, *admiral*! I do believe you are blushing!"

It only made it worse and he let go of her hand. "Julia, when we are finished with this little safari, I want that date."

"We'll see, admiral." she said.

"Senior chief, Actually."

"Yes, I know. I've seen your file," she said with a smile, and walked away.

CHAPTER 26

Operation Jimmy

Director Holstrom had named the operation "Jimmy" for his friend James McKnight. The men understood the significance and were refocused on the mission now that the school was built and they had a few days to adjust to the humidity and heat. It was after ten at night, and the men, plus Julia and Theresa, sat on the wooden floor of the school with a few ancient kerosene lamps.

Julia had a large map of the immediate area, which they were comparing to the GPS maps on their small computers. While the technical information on the satellite maps, in terms of longitudes and latitudes, was much more accurate, Julia's map showed local information that didn't appear on the CIA's map. Swamps, impassible jungles, ravines and other natural obstacles were identified in Julia's handwriting—information gathered from her Guaranis over the past two years. Unfortunately, the information only went into the jungle so far. The Guaranis that Julia knew did not like too venture too close to the Pampidos. The Pampidos were a rough bunch under any circumstances, but took exception to other Guaranis that chose to live in the cities with those who destroyed their forest. More than one Guarani had disappeared while traveling through the jungles near Pampidos lands.

Julia pointed to the Parana River on her map, at the Brazil-Paraguay border. "You can move by boat about thirty miles down the Parana to this point here. You'll travel faster in an hour than you will in half a day in the jungle." She pointed to another location down the river. "At this point, you would head west into the jungle. My people have only gone back five or six miles into the jungle there. It is extremely thick, with swamps and thorny patches of jungle that are literally impassable. We think that Vega has his camp somewhere in this general area, which gives him access to a few trails that lead both south into Argentina, and east into Brazil. None of my people have ever seen Vega or his Pampidos, but my Guaranis tell me they have seen Pampidos signs."

"What kind of signs?" asked Mackey.

"Warnings. Some of my Guaranis were scouting for me a couple of months back and came across some skulls mounted in the middle of a trail. They turned back immediately and wouldn't return. They are superstitious, but it was more than that—they were terrified."

"Of the skulls?" asked Mackey.

"Of what the Pampidos would do if they caught them. Cannibalism is only part of the nightmare. They can be extremely cruel to their prisoners before they kill and eat them." She paused. "So don't get caught." She looked at Cascaes when she said that, feeling a little pang.

Cascaes cleared his throat and looked at Mackey. "So we are just supposed to wander around in miserable jungle with no actual heading until we find someone who looks like a terrorist or cannibal?"

"Not exactly," said Julia. "Like I said, we do have some trails that may lead you towards his camp. I have the location of the warning signs—here," she said, pointing to the map. "My guess is when you get there, you'll be getting close. Oh, and another thing, if you can move at night, do it. The Pampidos are scared of the animal spirits that roam the jungle at night. They don't like moving after dark. You'd have a great advantage."

"We have plenty of night vision toys," said Mackey. He studied the map for a minute, comparing hers to his. "How long did it take your scouts to get to the point where they saw the skulls?"

"It was two days from where they got off the river. But they weren't moving very fast; they were mapping the area for me. My guess is you could do it in a day if you hustled. Just remember that what *they* call a trail around here is almost *invisible*. The plants grow back as fast as you can chop them with a machete. It's easy to get lost out there."

Mackey pointed at Cascaes. "I've got compass-boy over here to make sure we don't get lost." He looked at Cascaes. "Tomorrow morning? We could head out on the river and get down there by late morning. Then we shake a leg to the last mapped point where the skulls were located by dark. Quick break, and then off into the scary jungle at night. That work for you?"

Cascaes shrugged. "Sounds like an adventure. I should bring my camera."

Mackey and Cascaes spent the next hour going over details and equipment checklists with the men, who cleaned and inspected their weapons. Eric Hodges was checking his sniper rifle when he saw Mackey cleaning his Mossberg 590 shotgun. It was the "compact cruiser" edition, with a pistol grip instead of a rifle stock, and had a canvas strap attached to the pump for better speed and function on the run. Hodges laughed out loud.

"Hey skipper, what the hell are you gonna do with *that* thing?"

"You have your favorite gun, and I have mine. And I only have to be *close* with this sumbitch. I can pump off nine rounds in seven seconds, and I guarantee I *will* hit *something!*" He laughed.

"Yeah, well I know how those things are for accuracy, so do me a favor and make sure I'm not standing in front of you."

"Just remember this conversation when you're in the jungle and, scope or not, you can't see more then twenty feet," said Mackey, still smiling.

As the team finished cleaning and packing, Theresa returned with a backpack filled with first aid supplies. "You guys are lucky I love Julia, because going into that jungle at night is not my idea of a good time. And don't get hurt, because I'm much better at giving immunizations than I am at doing surgery in the field." She looked at Moose. "And I sure as shit ain't carrying *your* fat ass out of the jungle."

Moose bowed, still sharpening his black Ka-Bar combat knife. "I will try and keep that in mind, doc."

Theresa opened her backpack and started pulling out small bottles and syringes. "You knuckleheads should have had shots for the past four weeks to do this correctly, but some is better than none, so line up and 'drop trou.'"

Earl Jones saw the doctor filling a syringe and cringed. Hardened marine or not, shots made him queasy. "Uh, what's that for, doc?"

"I'm giving you shots for yellow fever, malaria and assorted other jungle bugs. You'll probably all have the shits the entire time you are running through the jungle, but I have pills for that, too." She smiled as she saw the room full of tough guys looking like a bunch of scared little boys.

"Line up!" she commanded.

Mackey pulled up his short sleeve, first to volunteer to set the example.

"No, sir. I said drop trou. These have to be given in the gluteus maximus."

Julia looked away to hide her face. She had seen Theresa give thousands of these shots to the Guaranis, but never once in any place other than the arm.

Theresa immunized the entire team and began putting her kit away.

"Hey wait, doc. You better give Miss Julia over there a shot, too. Let's see her drop trou," yelled Moose with a laugh.

"I've had mine, thank you very much," said Julia. "Although I do believe I got mine in the arm, didn't I, Theresa?"

Theresa smiled broadly. "Come to think of it, you might be right. These shots can be given in the arm after all." She turned back towards the men, who were laughing and groaning. "The truth is fellas, I don't get out much. This is the most ass I've seen in two years, thank you very much. And it would be very tough to pick a winner in the nicest ass contest." She walked over and slapped Moose as hard as she could where she had given him the shot. "Although I have to say that big boy over here almost bent my needle." She faked blowing him a kiss and walked away laughing.

The men unrolled sleeping bags and mosquito nets and got ready to grab some sleep. Julia and Teresa said goodnight and headed off to another small hut. Cascaes tried to quietly follow Julia out.

"You sure you don't want to stay in your new building?"

"I don't kiss on the first date, admiral. And I especially don't have sex in front of a dozen strangers with someone I just met. Call me old fashioned." She was playing with him, not being snotty.

"Yeah, well, when I get back, I want that date."

"I told you—we'll see." She walked back to him and planted a kiss full on his mouth. "But that will give you something to think about tonight while you are lying under the stars with your buddies." She turned and trotted after Theresa, leaving Chris standing by himself in shock. He smiled and shook his head as he watched her perfect little butt run out of sight.

As he turned to walk back inside, Mackey was standing there grinning. "Looks like you beat me to the prize," he said. "That is one of the most stunning women I have ever seen."

"Yeah, no shit," said Cascaes. "And don't frag my ass so you can go out with her, either!" He smacked Mackey and laughed, and they headed back inside to catch some sleep. The two of them laughed as they looked down on fifteen men in Ministry t-shirts with enough ammunition and weapons to start World War Three.

Mackey sat down and called Langley to tell them they would be starting Operation Jimmy tomorrow morning.

CHAPTER 27

Vega's Camp

Hakim Bin-Salaam was pacing back and forth in Vega's cabin. Vega himself was down at the coke barn, where the women were chopping and packing the dried leaves.

"How much longer do we have to rot here in this Godforsaken jungle?" he asked.

Ali Aziz, an older and calmer man, sat stroking his gray beard and clucked his tongue. "Patience, my brother. If we are caught at the airport, then all of our plans go up in smoke. I know you are not afraid to be a martyr, Hakim, but Allah still has plans for you on this earth, blessed be his name."

Raman Qasim, who had spent much more time in South America than the other two also tried to sooth his anxious comrade. "Hakim, it is not so bad, really, is it? We have brothers all over the world in much worse conditions than this, and they fight on bravely, do they not?"

Hakim nodded. "Yes, of course. I just hate the cursed bugs and the food here is not edible."

Ali raised a finger. "The fish was good. Perhaps we can ask the savages to get us some more."

Hakim grunted. "At least with the fish we know what we are eating. I think these animals eat everything they see. Serpents, monkeys, insects..."

"And each other," added Raman.

The other two just looked at each other.

"Like I said," grumbled Hakim, "The sooner we're out of this place, the better."

⊕

The morning was comparatively cool and comfortable, almost cold compared the scorching heat and humidity of full sun. The men woke up quietly and quickly started getting ready. They were still wearing their Los Angeles Ministries shirts, and their camos and weapons were packed in duffle bags and boxes marked with Red Cross emblems and first aid labels. They would be traveling down a wide river that had a fair amount of boat activity, although very little patrolling by any kind of police force.

Just in case, Mackey's Mossberg .590 would stay within easy reach, and several of the men had sidearms of various types tucked in their jeans. They headed down to the river and inflated the boats. As they were packing, Theresa showed up with her first aid kit, followed by Julia and a young Guarani man. He was dark and very small.

Julia saw Chris and smiled. He walked over to say goodbye.

"Goodbye? Not quite, darling. I thought our first date would be a jungle cruise. Sounds so romantic, don't you think?"

Chris smiled and said, "Very funny".

"No really, Chris. Theresa and I spoke last night. This is Fassissi. We just call him Fuzzy. He's been the deepest into the jungle. He wasn't keen on going back, but he said he'd go if I went with him, so there you are. We're all going on a little picnic."

"Fuzzy can come. You're staying," said Cascaes.

"Actually, you are not my boss, admiral. And I have jungle training just like you tough guys, *and* I know the area better than all of you combined. I'm not planning on going all the way to Vega's camp, anyway. I'll just take you in with Fuzzy to the last known location of the Pampidos signs."

"*Hey Mack!*" yelled Cascaes. "We have a little problem over here."

Mackey walked over to Cascaes. He had already spoken to Julia earlier in the morning. "Chris, if she is going to be a distraction, she can come in my boat. She's going as far as the map notes go. Then Fuzzy will bring her back to the boats. So what will it be? My boat or yours?"

Cascaes looked at Julia, who made her sexiest pouty face.

"Jesus Christ. You're gonna' get us all killed." He started walking towards his boat. "Well don't just stand there, grab your gear and let's get moving."

Moose walked over, picked Julia up like a small child, and placed her carefully inside the large black rubber raft. She looked at Cascaes, who was looking at her and shaking his head, but cracked a smile.

She saw the smile and pointed at him, yelling "Ha!"

He just said "shut up" under his breath and hopped into the raft.

The two boats were heading downstream in a fairly good current, and they used their oars to save the batteries for the return trip using their small electric outboard motors. The outboards were electric so they could run silently, but this limited the engines to about three hours at full power, which was twenty-two knots. Mackey was in boat one with Fuzzy, Theresa and seven of his men. Cascaes had ten on his boat as well. With ten passengers each and equipment, the boats were packed like sardines, but it added to the authenticity of their cover story—two boatloads of missionaries heading out to help the natives.

The river was quiet early in the morning. The water was brownish green and still as glass in most parts. It continually grew wider and deeper, and eventually, other boats would occasionally come into view for a short time, but no one paid much attention to the two small rafts. Cascaes was sitting up front next to Julia, and they were both very much aware of the contact their thighs were making against each other in the small raft.

Neither of them were paddling, they were simply enjoying the ride while the others did the work. Rank had its occasional privileges, and besides, they didn't have ten oars for each boat.

Julia leaned over and quietly said, "Good thing we're in the front of the boat, huh? You'd probably try and cop a feel."

He pressed against her thigh with his own. "I *am* copping a feel," he said quietly.

"You only bring me to the nicest places," she replied.

He just looked at her, enjoying her company, but not particularly happy she was along. She was a major distraction and this wasn't a cakewalk.

"What the hell are you doing here, anyway?" he asked. "I mean really? You could be anywhere doing anything, why this dark corner of the earth?"

"I think you saw part of the reason. Your men were practically ready to stay and play with the children forever themselves. I've been an agent in different parts of the world, doing all types of missions. This cover story became a real life to me. The people I help have no one else in the world, and for the first time I can really see results of my work. Do you know how much better it feels to help a child than kill an adult?"

Cascaes exhaled slowly. "Yeah, I guess so," he said quietly.

"Hey," she added, "I'm not judging you or what you do. You and your men are soldiers and do what needs to be done. It's honorable to serve your country like you do. I've done my share of killing, too."

That brought a look of surprise from Cascaes, then simple admiration. This woman could quite literally do anything— from runway model to assassin. It was intriguing to say the least.

"It's just that the last job," he said very quietly. "Two little kids...well, it was an accident, sort of. I mean, we didn't know they were there, but I think we would have had to kill them

anyway. It was messed up. I had managed to block it out, but
what you said just now made it pop back into my head. It
sucked."

She patted his thigh, and Moose, who was two rows back,
saw her hand.

"Hey!" he yelled, "This is a family cruise! Keep your hands
in your own lap!"

Both Chris and Julia held up a one-finger salute, as if they
had rehearsed it for hours, and then laughed at each other.

"You're okay," he said quietly.

"You, too," she said softly, and slowly removed her hand.

CHAPTER 28

The Jungle

It was three o'clock in the afternoon when they arrived at a small bend in the river where a tiny tributary broke off to the north. They paddled into it and continued upstream until the stream became a creek, and very shallow. Fuzzy hopped off the raft without warning and quickly walked towards the dense jungle growth. He would occasionally squat down and look closely at the ground and at the rocks, trying to find familiar landmarks, as the men landed the two rafts and quickly began unloading.

They worked silently, pulling the gear into the jungle and out of sight as fast as possible. Within a minute, all of them had their yellow shirts off and replaced them with jungle camouflage. They broke out their commando face paint kits, and within a few minutes were all colored an assortment of greens, browns and blacks. Their bright yellow shirts and assorted tennis shoes were bagged up and thrown into the boats, and they pulled on socks and their waterproof jungle boots. Once weapons were assembled and computers and radios were checked out, they pulled the boats into the jungle a little deeper and deflated them, then buried them after turning on their GPS tracking devices.

Julia and Theresa watched in silence, amazed at the speed with which the men worked. Chris walked over with his grease paint and smiled at Julia, his own face mostly green and black.

"Seems like such a shame," he said, and he put a smear of green paint across her cheek.

"I can do my own make-up," she said with a smile.

"No, ma'am. This has to be done to Navy regulations," he said quietly, and continued to paint her face slowly and carefully. The way he was touching her face made her blush under the green, brown and black streaks. Luckily, the others were too busy to pay any attention.

Moose walked over to Theresa and was going to attempt the same smooth move, but she swiped the can from him and said, "Don't even *think* about it, pal." When she saw his hurt face, she lightened up. "How's that ass doing?" she asked with a smile.

"Still the nicest one in the navy," he replied.

Theresa stuck out her own rear end and said, "You wish."

That got her a smile, and she hustled off to grab her backpack.

Once everyone was geared up, they took a knee in a small circle around Mackey and Cascaes.

Mackey spoke quietly. "Okay, show-time, boys and girls. Julia, does Fuzzy have anything yet?" She spoke in Guarani to him, and he answered back and started walking into the jungle.

"I told him we'd follow him. If he goes too fast, just let me know," said Julia.

"Okay everybody, single file. Santos on point, Woods—backdoor. Stay together people. No one get off the fucking trail and make sure you can see the person in front of you at all times. It is going to get thick out there in a little while. Everybody turn on their trackers."

All of the team members had been given small devices that would locate them by satellite if they were lost or injured and couldn't call for help. Santos checked his MP5 and hustled after Fuzzy, followed by Cascaes and Mackey. Moose was next, followed by Theresa and Julia, and then the rest of the team filed behind them.

Santos was amazed at how Fuzzy moved through the jungle. He didn't hack his way through the jungle with a machete; he glided like he was floating, totally relaxed and noiseless. Fuzzy wore only a loincloth, not even sandals. Mackey saw him move through the large leaves and remembered his days in Vietnam, where the sappers could move through the jungle like that.

No one spoke, they just walked briskly single file, lost in their own thoughts, constantly watching everything around them. An hour into the hike, Santos gave a quiet "psssst!" to Fuzzy and motioned him to stop. They took a knee for some water and to wipe off their faces. All of them were completely soaked. It wasn't as hot as the dessert, but it was so humid you could see the water vapor in the filtered sunlight of the jungle. They were finishing their water break when Ernie P. started slapping his legs like a wild-man.

Woods, who was behind him, jumped up and grabbed him, then saw what he was doing. Ernie had taken a knee on an ant mound, and was now under attack by hundreds of pissed-off stinging ants. As soon as Woods started pulling them off, Koches joined in and helped them, slapping and pulling off the soldier ants, whose large jaws had locked onto Ernie's skin. He was doing his best to stay quiet, but the ants were everywhere. They eventually dragged him a few yards up the trail, away from the mound, and spent the next ten minutes killing ants and then spraying his red welts with antiseptic from Theresa's kit.

She leaned over to him and quietly said, "If you start feeling funky, tell me and I'll give you a shot of antihistamine—but only if you need it. It will make you tired."

He replied that he was okay, and thanked her, then took his spot back in the single file line. Mackey reiterated to "keep your eyes open" because there would be more bugs and snakes and things to make you miserable up ahead. Fuzzy appeared out of nowhere next to Ernie and gave him what looked like greenish-brown, foul-smelling goo from Lord-knows-where, and motioned for him to rub it on his bites. Ernie did so, reluctantly, but the stinging was gone instantly. He smiled at Fuzzy, who recognized the universal language of a smile, and patted his arm. Fuzzy glided back to the front of the group and continued leading them on their journey.

The team continued silently and without incident for another four hours, stopping twice to drink and once for a quick MRE to recharge a bit. The sun was now getting lower and disappearing behind the top of the tree canopy. The sounds of the jungle began changing, as the day creatures and night creatures began their shift rotation. Fuzzy walked back to Julia and began chattering away quietly. They conversed for a quite a while, bringing Mackey and Cascaes over to wait for the outcome of the mysterious conversation. When Fuzzy was finished, Julia turned to the two Chrises.

"Fuzzy says we're getting close to where the Pampidos had left their warnings. It will be dark soon, and he's getting a little stressed." She smiled. "I am paraphrasing."

Cascaes pulled out his small computer and pulled up the GIS map. He compared his present location on the map with the notes on Julia's map. "Julia, according to your map notes, and our present location, we aren't that close yet. Maybe another two and half miles. Does he understand miles?"

Julia smiled through her camouflage paint. "Not only doesn't he understand miles the way we do, he doesn't understand time, either. These guys aren't big on past, present and future tenses. It gets very confusing. Unless they are talking about a story from the ancestors, I never know exactly how much time we are talking about."

"Great," mumbled Cascaes. "Ask him why he thinks we're close."

Julia repeated it back to him, and he responded by climbing a tree. They all looked at each other.

"You mind telling me what the fuck he is doing?" asked Mackey, hot, tired and cranky.

"I have no idea," said Julia.

Fuzzy disappeared for what felt like a long time, up into the canopy. When he reappeared, he was carrying a dead monkey.

"What the hell..." Cascaes started to say, and then he watched Fuzzy pull out a small wooden dart with green feathers attached to it. Fuzzy chattered away at Julia for a moment, then stopped and started examining the monkey.

Julia scratched her head. "I have no idea how he does that. Little Fuzzy over here says that the Pampidos were hunting here. Apparently, they hit this little guy with a blow-dart but he managed to escape and die up in the tree. I asked Fuzzy how he knew the monkey was up there, and I take it from his nasty explanation, that when the monkey died from the poison in the dart, which they get from blue tree frogs, by the way, they tend to shit their little brains out. He saw a nice spray of monkey poop all over the trees and leaves and knew what had happened immediately. He wants to know if he can keep the monkey. I told him yes."

"Holy shit," said Mackey.

"No pun intended," said Cascaes quietly.

"Okay, so the Pampidos have been out this far, but this is still pretty far from the warning signs, right?" asked Cascaes.

Julia shrugged. "I have no idea. Right now, Fuzzy is happy to have his favorite food, but it will start getting dark soon, and he is going to get skittish about continuing on in the dark."

"We can give him night vision," said Cascaes.

"Chris! Are you out of your mind? You let him see glowing images in the dark and he will die of a heart attack. These guys are scared of night spirits. Night vision will definitely put him over the edge." She folded her arms. "So now what?"

"So now our little friend and his monkey take you back to the boat and you go home. I'll send one of the guys back with you to help with the raft. We'll call you by radio when you can come back with the boat," said Cascaes.

"Oh, I don't think so," she snapped back.

"It isn't a request, ma'am. We are going to be going into combat tomorrow or the next day. It's bad enough we have Theresa along—not a sexist comment—but she hasn't trained with us at all. This is no time to start bringing in new personnel."

"Look, admiral, you are going to need every member of your team, and Fuzzy is going to be a huge help tomorrow when you need to find the Pampidos territory border. He is better in the jungle than any one of your men—so admit it and stop thinking you have to baby-sit. I did the course at Langley, too."

Mackey put his hand up before Chris could answer. "Stand down senior chief. She's right. I don't want to lose any of our crew if we can help it. Julia has kept up as well as any of the men. When it's time to assault, we can keep her and Theresa out of direct combat. And Fuzzy has been amazing. He's better than the damn computers or a bloodhound. I think we should keep moving until he won't go any further, then find a place to overnight. We'll move out real early and push hard tomorrow."

Cascaes didn't like it, but it wasn't his call, and he also recognized that he was feeling slightly overprotective beyond professional feelings. When they went back to Fuzzy to tell him they wanted him to go forward, they found him squatting over the monkey, its head opened with his knife. He was happily eating the brains. Cascaes and Mackey looked at each other and grimaced. Fuzzy smiled and offered some to them on his fingertips, which was very generous since it was his favorite food. They politely declined. Julia explained that when he was finished, they wanted to keep moving forward. They chatted back and forth for a while, and finally Julia explained that he had agreed to keep going for a while more—just as soon as he was finished with dinner.

No human ear would have been sensitive enough to hear the slightest rustling of leaves as three Pampidos hunters melted back into the jungle, then began running like shadows towards their small village only a few kilometers away.

CHAPTER 29

Nightfall, in the Jungle

Fuzzy had led them for another few kilometers on the trail that was visible apparently only to him. Cascaes continuously checked their location against his GPS computer and relayed that location back to Langley where Dex Murphy was being updated every hour or so on their progress. As dusk turned to twilight, Fuzzy began getting nervous. Even though he hadn't lived in the jungle like the "wild Guaranis", he still believed in the animal spirits that came out at night. Fuzzy worked his way back to Julia and told her it was time to find a shelter.

She relayed the information back to Mackey, who called Cascaes over to confer. They both wanted to keep moving for another few hours, and Julia tried pleading with Fuzzy. He was looking genuinely frightened, and refused. The two Chrises decided that Fuzzy was too valuable to leave, and that whatever time they lost by stopping early would be made up by Fuzzy's expert guide service the next morning.

Fuzzy began his clicking and chattering with Julia for a bit, and she explained to Mackey and Cascaes that he needed to build a shelter to keep the spirits out. They helped him cut down a few very large leaves and ripped some huge pieces of bark from giant trees. They surrounded Fuzzy with the bark "walls" and placed leaves over his one-person apartment, and he curled up on the mossy ground and went to sleep. The team looked at each other, somewhat perplexed and entertained, and then set about securing a perimeter.

Raul Santos and Ernie P. moved quietly through the jungle together, weapons at the ready, and placed small computer sensors in a fifty-yard perimeter around their location in twenty-yard intervals. Anything that either moved or generated heat and weighed more than fifty pounds would light up on their small computer. They didn't set booby-traps or claymores and would remain silent if possible.

After a dinner of cold MRE's and some quiet conversation, the team set out small tarps with zip-up sleeping bags the purpose of which was simply to remain dry and free of insects. Cascaes took first watch with Smitty and everyone else tried to steal a few hours of sleep, weapons loaded and within reach. The quality of sleep one got in this jungle would be different than in the Everglades.

Chris made some instant coffee, which he drank cold, since they didn't light a fire. He was sitting on a smooth rock, covered with thick green moss that made a comfortable seat. He smiled when Julia sat down next to him and pushed against his hip with her own.

"Move over, admiral," she whispered. "You're hogging the whole thing."

He smiled and felt himself blush. She had a funny effect on him. "There is *no* talking on watch. I bet you can't last three minutes." He stared into her eyes. Even covered with commando face paint she was beautiful, with high cheekbones and thick eyelashes.

She smiled and returned his gaze, then crossed her arms and made it a staring contest. After what seemed like a long time, she held up one finger—she was counting. They continued their contest until she raised her second finger, then her third. Cascaes leaned over and whispered into her ear.

"You win," he whispered so quietly she could hardly hear, and then lightly kissed her neck.

Julia felt goose bumps on her arms, which she looked down to inspect, then showed them to Chris.

"Nice," she whispered. "I think it's been a while."

She leaned over and kissed him full on the mouth, then whispered, "Goodnight." She pulled his floppy jungle hat down playfully and stood up.

He watched her work herself into her thin sleeping bag, then cover herself up completely with the mosquito netting. She got herself as comfortable as possible, lying next to Theresa, and smiled to herself as she thought about her attraction to the navy SEAL only a few yards away.

The team rotated shifts throughout the night, allowing each man a few hours sleep. Though they monitored the computer all night, there was no activity beyond the sounds of the jungle at night.

CHAPTER 30

Vega's Camp

The three Pampidos hunters ran the entire way back to their village from where they had spotted the soldiers. They had only seen six of Mackey's crew, but knew from their camouflage uniforms and weapons it wouldn't be wise to attack them without help. They ran through the village straight to Kuka's oga, where they entered and knelt prone before their abrubicha, panting like racehorses.

Kuka, who was sitting with one of his wives when they entered, walked to his men and told them to speak. They reported seeing soldiers, who they thought were white men painted green to try and be invisible like them. They had seen six, and they appeared to be heading towards their village.

Kuka told the men to eat and rest, a compliment to their work, and headed out to find Enrique, whom he knew would not be happy. The last time white men came close to their camp, Vega had made Kuka take all of his warriors and Vega's soldiers to find them. There had been three of them, and they fought hard when attacked. One of them had been able to escape, even though he had been wounded many times. The other two had been killed, but only after seven of Kuka's men had also been killed. The Guaranis honored their enemies by eating them that evening over the campfires. Their skulls now served as a warning to others who would dare to venture too close to their village.

129

Kuka found Vega sitting with the three men who had been in and out of their village several times, but did not live there. He interrupted their conversation and began speaking too quickly for Vega to understand. After the third time, Vega's face fell.

"You are sure? Soldiers are headed here? How far, Kuka?" he asked angrily.

Kuka counted to six, but time and distance was always tricky. Vega was guessing they were only a day away at most.

Vega turned to his Arab guests, his face red with anger.

"I told you your bombing would bring soldiers here!" screamed Vega.

He rarely raised his voice to the Arabs, but his anger had gotten the best of him. "If I have to move this damn village again, so help me God…" He stood and starting pacing. He pointed at Raman, whom he considered the leader. "This is *your* fault, Raman! I've got half a dozen soldiers coming here now—probably Americans, too."

Raman's face tightened. He wasn't used to being spoken to in such a manner, and all three of the Arabs were miserable hiding out in the jungle to begin with. Their moods were already sour.

"Calm yourself, Señor Vega," said Raman through clenched teeth. "First of all, there are only six of them. You must have over a hundred savages here, plus your own men. You'll deal with them like you did last time."

Vega was furious now. "*Last* time I almost had Kuka quit on me after a bunch of his men were machine gunned. Then I had to move my entire operation deeper into this godforsaken jungle and add another day to our coke shipments. It cost me a lot of money, Raman."

Ali Aziz, always calm and methodical, sat twirling his beard as usual. "Calm, Señor Vega. We must all remain calm. We will pay you for any inconvenience. You will find these soldiers and kill them. No one will ever find them, and your camp can remain right where it is. We will get you some extra weapons next trip to make sure you are properly protected. And I doubt that these are Americans, anyway. They have no reason to be here. The soldiers are probably Paraguayan police, pressured to make a show of force. You won't have too much trouble."

Vega tried to calm himself and contemplated that. "Perhaps," he said, "but they are only a day or so away. We need to get organized immediately." He stood up and spoke to Kuka, and the two of them left their Arab comrades in the hut as they set off to organize their small army.

Kuka found a small boy and spoke quickly to him, sending the boy to the center of the village to begin pounding on a large drum that would bring all of the warriors running. Vega jogged down to the coke barn, where a few of his men sat outside smoking and playing cards. He told them that there were soldiers coming, and they immediately scrambled to find the others. Within ten minutes, all ten of Vega's men had their AK-47s loaded and were down by the village. Kuka's warriors had assembled and awaited instructions.

Vega walked into the center of the village with his men behind him and approached Kuka. He spoke to him in Guarani, appealing to his pride and warrior mentality. He loudly called upon the Great abrubicha Kuka to assemble only his bravest warriors to fight the intruders. He would need them to be great fighters, fast and fearless, to attack those that would destroy their homes and kill their women and children. It was a decent enough speech to work the men into a frenzy, and the drums began almost immediately, followed by whistles and singing from the women.

Kuka ordered his men to prepare, which meant painting themselves and putting on their feathers, stringing their large bows, and preparing their poison arrows. They would gather their weapons, eat a hearty dinner of meat, and then take off silently into their jungle to kill anyone that dared entered their territory.

Vega walked back to his cabin followed by his men, knowing they would need a few minutes for the Guaranis to be in full battle dress. Besides being fearless warriors, they had the ability to scare the shit out of their enemies by merely showing up—over one hundred natives, painted red and green, with small feathers tied in their hair. Bones and animal teeth were pushed through their earlobes, noses and lower lips, and their stone-age weapons looked as menacing as any AK-47 up close.

Vega's men had put together backpacks full of ammunition, water and smoked meats, fish, and plant roots. They pulled their packs on and made sure their weapons were loaded and ready, then assembled in front of Vega. Carlos, one of Vega's best men, asked if there was any specific plan. Vega told Carlos to leave behind two men with him, and take everyone else to follow the Guaranis back to where they spotted the intruders.

The three Arabs watched silently as the men prepared to move out. Then Raman broke the silence. "Perhaps we should consider having a few of your men lead us back to the river. It might be a good time to try and get to the airport, if the police are more concerned with the jungle."

Vega looked at him and resisted the urge to call him a coward and slit his throat.

"No, Raman. You started this mess. You'll stay here until it is over."

Ali Aziz, seeing Vega's anger seething, said, "Of course, Señor Vega. We will stay until the situation has been taken care of. I'm sure it will only be another day or so, and then we will be out of your hair."

Vega ignored him and walked out followed by his men. He told Carlos to keep an eye on them and make sure they didn't try and make a run for it. He didn't trust them, and their little business arrangement of convenience was beginning to look less attractive. Carlos and three men stayed in camp with the Guarani women and children, and a handful of older men. The rest of the men were painted and prepared for battle and sat chewing coca leaves.

Kuka emerged from his oga, looking quite impressive. His head was encircled with orange feathers, and his body was covered in painted green polka dots. He carried his alligator tooth-lined club and had a knife tucked in his loincloth. Long porcupine quills had been inserted through his nose making him look even fiercer. He shouted to his warriors, who shouted back and began chanting, now high on coca leaves. The three young hunters who had spotted the soldiers trotted out into the jungle to lead the way, followed by Kuka and his warriors, who brandished clubs, spears, knives, large bows and arrows and blowguns. Vega's men followed the seemingly endless line of warriors into the jungle.

Within a few moments, the Guaranis had gone silent, and trotted through the woods without making the slightest noise. They were invisible, and headed for battle.

CHAPTER 31

Mornings were loud in the Paraguayan jungle. The birds weren't singing, they were *screaming*. So were the monkeys and various other animals that scampered overhead in the giant double canopy of ancient trees. The sun was barely up, and already the jungle had exploded into activity. Moose had been up early, and dug a deep pit where he burned some sterno to boil water for coffee. No longer worried about light giving away their position, the tiny fire was safe, since it didn't produce much smoke.

Everyone stood slowly, putting away their gear and checking weapons, then moving towards the smell of coffee. Moose had made enough for everyone and poured some into a small cup, which he brought to Theresa.

She smiled through tired eyes and thanked him, then sipped the very strong coffee. "Yup," she said, "Same recipe the marines use for mud."

Julia leaned towards her and said, "I think he *likes* you, likes you."

She rolled her eyes. "Yeah, well don't think I don't see what's going on with you and *your* little friend over there, sister. You getting soft on me?"

Julia smiled, her teeth very white against the smeared paint on her face. "*Maybe*," she said softly.

"Oh, God," moaned Theresa. "You're a goner. *This* is a first."

Their conversation was interrupted by Cascaes—speak of the devil—calling out softly to his men.

"Okay everybody, listen up. We are going to stay together for another mile or so, then we should be getting very close. At the appropriate place, we'll split into three groups. The main group will stay on the trail behind Fuzzy and try and find the village. The other two teams will take our flanks and move out about two hundred yards. Team one will be Hodges, Santos, Smitty, and McCoy on the left flank. If possible, Hodges will find a position to set up his sniper rifle and cover the village from the west side as the main body comes in from the south. Mackey will take team two on the right flank with Woods, Koches, Stewart and O'Conner. Assuming we find the village undetected, we will stay silent until dark. The Guaranis don't like moving at night, as Fuzzy can attest to, and I doubt Vega's men have night vision equipment. We'll go in quiet, silencers on, and take out Vega and all of his men. If we get lucky and find that the terrorist targets are there as well, we'll take them out, too. Avoid contact with the natives if you can help it. They are dangerous, but they aren't our objective. If they run, do not pursue. I'd just as soon have them take off into the jungle and not fight them at all. If all goes well and we take out the targets, we'll rig whatever drug operations he has going out there with explosives as we exit.

"Everyone make sure your locators are working, check your throat mics, and make sure you stay with a buddy like you were on a dive mission. Nobody goes off alone out here, understand? The jungle is only going to get thicker up ahead and if you get lost out here, you're fucked. Everybody clear?"

The team members nodded, and assembled their silencers to their weapons. Mackey slung his shotgun over his back, since it was deafening and didn't have a silencer. He pulled an MP-5 "Room Broom" out of his backpack, slapped in a thirty-round magazine, and fitted a silencer.

Cascaes put on his throat mic and began checking each team member's reception. As he said their names, one at a time, they each confirmed that they heard him. He then opened a small laptop and pulled up a screen that showed a map grid and numbered circles in a tight blob. Each number was a team member, located by the small tracking device they wore. Cascaes checked in with Langley, gave their location, and reported that their locators and communication equipment were now "live." While CIA headquarters couldn't see them by satellite, they could follow the team by locators and listen in on their transmissions.

Fuzzy led them back up the trail, which was visible only to him, and they stayed together single file and silent. The jungle was changing as they walked, from well-spaced giant trees with under-story growth and soft ferns, to thick spiny vines, giant alien looking shrubs with bright flowers and razor sharp thorns, and heavy vines that hung everywhere. It was losing the "forest" feel, and becoming more ominous. Even Fuzzy had to slow down as he maneuvered around plants designed to destroy skin.

The air was thick with humidity again, and giant insects were everywhere. The most brilliant azure butterflies would fill the sky one minute, attracted by some bright flower, and then a cloud of buzzing flies or mosquitoes would descend the next. The team eventually stopped to spray DEET all over themselves in an attempt to hide from the mosquitoes, but it was fairly useless. Fuzzy pointed out an eleven foot anaconda wrapped in a tree, a huge lump in its belly from something it had eaten in the last few days. Whatever it had been, it made a bulge in the snake's midsection that was as big as Fuzzy.

Once, Julia had picked an orange flower off a bush and handed it to Cascaes when no one was watching. He tried to look like a hard-ass and put his finger over his mouth to remind her to remain silent, and she responded by blowing him a silent kiss. He shook his head and shoved the flower in his pocket. Each of them knew the other was going to be trouble if they didn't get killed first.

By midday, the team came to a small creek and watched in amazement as Fuzzy got down on all fours like a dog to lap up the water. He didn't even use his hands to cup the water, he just shoved his face into the stream and drank. Mackey let everyone take a break and eat a meal replacement bar. He offered one to Fuzzy, who smelled it, turned up his nose, and instead pulled a caterpillar off of a rotting log and ate it. Half way through, he realized his rudeness, and offered it to Mackey, who politely declined.

Theresa happened to see the incident and whispered, "Oh, go ahead, they taste like almonds." He just looked at her and waved his power bar.

After a quick drink from their canteens, and a few quick trips into the bushes for personal moments, the team was back on the trail, which was now very thick mud. Fuzzy spoke quietly to Julia, who whispered to Mackey that they were very close to where the Pampidos warning signs had been. They walked through the greenish brown ooze, pulling their boots out of each step as they went. Somehow Fuzzy managed to stay on top of the mud, while everyone else fought to keep from being sucked to their knees. It was exhausting, and they were all very relieved when they reach a small bank that was dry. Fuzzy squatted and turned to Julia, shaking his head. Mackey didn't have to ask—this was as far as Fuzzy wanted to go. Fuzzy whispered to Julia, and then turned back and disappeared into the jungle. It was the end of the road for him.

Mackey motioned to Cascaes, who was team leader when it came to combat. Cascaes held up one finger and Team One quietly spread out to the left flank and crawled up to peer over the bank. Cascaes then held up a second finger, and Mackey took his men to the right, also inching up the bank to see what was waiting for them.

Santos, in Team One, was the first one up the embankment, and slowly raised his face to peer over the edge. The jungle opened up quite a bit, allowing sunlight into a small rocky clearing. He belly crawled forward and stopped in some giant leaves, then pulled out his small binoculars. He scanned for a few seconds before he saw what had scared Fuzzy away the last trip.

Two long poles stood at the other side of the clearing. Each of them had a head affixed to the top, the pole having been shoved through the bottom jaw. The skulls hadn't been boiled out to nice clean white bone, but had instead been festering and feeding the bugs. The hair hung matted from the decayed heads, and as Santos focused clearer, he could see that genitalia, presumably from one of the poor victims, had been shoved into the mouth of one of the skulls. The other skull had a large opening near the top where the victim had apparently suffered a major fracture. Looking farther along the tree line, he saw other body parts and objects hanging from trees, tied against other branches and poles. For someone like Fuzzy, it was the equivalent of a giant billboard that said "turn around and start running."

Santos spoke quietly into his throat mic. "Team One to Jimmy Leader, I have Fuzzy's landmark in sight. Approximately one hundred yards across an open field at the opposite tree line. I would need to work around a few hundred yards to avoid crossing in the open. You want me to go? Over."

Cascaes told him to sit tight and went up the bank in front of him to see for himself. The rest of the team followed on their bellies. Mackey and Team Two continued to move to the right and eventually called back that they were two hundred yards to the right flank and could also see the clearing. Cascaes looked across the rocky clearing at the same rotting skulls that Santos had seen. He passed the binoculars to his men so they would know who they were dealing with.

"Okay, Santos," said Cascaes, "move to your left and work your way over. Hodges, get your sniper rifle set up and cover him from your present position. Everyone else stay put and keep your eyes open." Cascaes lay still on his belly with his binoculars, scanning the opposite tree line while trying to keep an eye on Santos.

CHAPTER 32

Kuka's warriors moved quickly and silently through the jungle, almost at a run. Vega's men struggled to keep up, huffing and puffing under the weight of their weapons and packs. Just when Vega's men were ready to collapse, the Guaranis stopped moving. It was amazing the way they could stop moving, crouch slightly into the leaves, and almost disappear in an instant. One of the warriors trotted ahead, followed by twenty or so men with large bows over their shoulders. They carried extremely large arrows—small spears really, and hustled after their leader.

The warriors moved quietly to the edge of a large rocky clearing and sat down, removing the large bows from their backs and placing them under their feet as they sat on their rear-ends. Holding the bows under their feet, they used both arms to pull back on the string and notch the giant arrow. In this manner, they could loose an arrow the size of a small spear and send it fifty yards with amazing accuracy. It was the same method they used for hunting birds, monkeys and anything else overhead. The single warrior that was the leader of this primitive platoon of archers belly-crawled silently towards the edge of the clearing. He couldn't see soldiers yet, but every ounce of his being sensed enemies nearby.

Behind the archers, the woods filled up with warriors, working their way loosely through the jungle towards the clearing. Vega's six men, armed with AK-47s, also moved forward, keeping an eye on Kuka to make sure they didn't get lost in the jungle.

$$\oplus$$

Santos worked his way around the fringe of the jungle, moving quietly through the large ferns. With his floppy hat and painted face, he was hard to spot, and Cascaes kept losing him from his position in the center of their group.

It wasn't a *noise* really—not a "sound" per se—but it was *something*. A subsonic buzz or hum, and then nothing for a second, and then almost a whistling noise. Santos froze and looked up. A cloud of spears was flying through the air in his direction, first flying almost straight up, and then descending upon his location in a tightening cloud. He was crawling on his belly when he saw them, and then the screaming in his earpiece began. "Look out!" Cascaes warned.

Santos started rolling as fast as he could down a slight embankment, and as he rolled, he worked his body into position to spring up and start running. Hodges, who saw the arrows appear from nowhere, still didn't have a target, but was screaming at Santos to run. Santos pushed off his hands and was ready to sprint when a spear landed in the back of his thigh and continued straight through into the ground, pinning him. Another dozen landed all around him, but miraculously didn't hit him. He was screaming when the spear impaled him into the soft jungle floor.

Smitty and McCoy began running around the edge of the jungle clearing to work their way over to their injured friend. They yelled to Cascaes that they were moving to help, and Cascaes yelled back to get him, but to stay out of the open. Mackey and his team didn't see Santos go down, but heard the commotion over their earpieces and double-timed it to work their way around the clearing from the right flank, moving towards an enemy they still hadn't seen yet. As they moved around to the right, Cascaes' team in the center spread out along the edge of the embankment, well concealed, trying to get visual targets across the clearing.

Theresa began running towards the left flank knowing that Santos was injured, and Moose called after her. "Where the hell do you think you're going?" he screamed as he tried to catch up to her.

"I'm a combat medic," she hollered back, ignoring him as she ran.

Cascaes heard them and yelled "Go!" to Moose, who ran with her through the woods. They were sprinting through thorny bushes, knocking over small trees as they ran, but ignored everything as they focused on getting towards Santos. Cascaes and his men had yet to return a shot, and the enemy was still unseen after the single flight of arrows.

Moose and Theresa came running up behind Hodges, who was concentrating on finding a target across the clearing through his sniper scope, and they startled him. He heard their footsteps running towards him from behind and whipped his .45 out of its holster and spun around.

"Don't shoot!" yelled Theresa, who kept running right past him along the tree line. Moose was right behind her, his MP-5 looking tiny in his huge hands. Hodges cursed under his breath and rolled back over, again trying to see an enemy target through his scope. He didn't have a spotter, which was the way he usually worked, and it was a handicap. Across the clearing, a painted face finally rose above the knee-high ferns. Hodges didn't know it, but it was the group leader of the archers, trying to find another target. Hodges squeezed off a round and removed the top of his head. It was the first bullet of the day.

Across the field, the Guaranis streamed through the woods towards their enemy. The crack of a rifle made them freeze only for a second—they squatted and disappeared into the ferns to reassess the threat.

McCoy was the first to reach Santos, who was crying out in pain and trying in vein to pull the huge pole out of his thigh that was pinned to the ground.

"Hang on, man!" said McCoy as he flopped on the ground between Santos and the unseen enemy. He ripped his pack off of his back and pulled out a first aid pack, tearing off a morphine syringe. "Just relax, man, I'm gonna' get you out of here."

Smitty thundered past them, shooting in short bursts in the general direction of the enemy, trying to suppress unseen targets.

"Pete! Hurry, man...*oh God...oh God...*" Santos was trying to be brave, but the pain was excruciating and he could feel his heart beat pounding in his thigh. McCoy popped the syringe into Santos' shoulder and scanned the immediate area. He called back to Cascaes.

"Team leader, this is McCoy. I have Santos and..." his voice trailed off and then he yelled, "Oh shit!" as another cloud of giant arrows was released in their direction. McCoy dove over Santos, snapping the pole that was through his leg and releasing him from the ground. Santos was screaming in agony. He grabbed Santos by his vest and heaved him off the ground and started running as the first spears began impacting around them. He ran and stumbled as Santos's legs tangling with his, sending them both sprawling. Santos grunted as he hit the ground, but the morphine was starting to kick in and put him out. As Pete pulled Santos through the ferns by his jacket, Theresa and Moose came sprinting through the woods.

"Hang on!" yelled Theresa as she ran towards them. Moose had his weapon at the ready, but still had no target. "Screw it!" he yelled, and began firing blindly in the direction the spears had come from. Across the clearing, his bullets quietly zipped through the plants and leaves, and the Guaranis squatted and disappeared again, untouched by the incoming rounds.

Theresa rolled Santos on his back and checked his pulse. He was unconscious but alive. The bleeding wasn't too bad because the large spear was still imbedded in the meaty part of his thigh.

"McCoy—you alright?" yelled Moose.

"Yeah, I'm good," he screamed back as he readied his weapon.

"Okay, you grab Raul and get the hell out of here with Theresa. I'll cover your withdrawal.

McCoy immediately threw his weapon to Theresa and pulled Santos over his shoulder in a fireman's carry. They took off in the same direction from which they came and Moose began backing up a few yards at a time, making sure they wouldn't be rushed. In the background, they could hear the occasional crack of Hodges' sniper rifle when he acquired a target.

Mackey's voice came in over the radio. "Jimmy leader, Team Two is preparing to assault!"

"Roger that Team Two, but don't get too far ahead of us. We can't offer much fire support from here. We can't see a damn thing. Ripper, Cohen and Jones, work your way around the right flank and come in behind Team Two. The rest of us will stay here for now and try and acquire targets while we wait for Santos."

Mackey and his four men had worked around the clearing and were now inching along through the ferns and underbrush. In front of them, the Guaranis were running towards the edge of the clearing, and working their way to their own right, evidently believing that Santos and the others were coming from that direction. Mackey and his men managed to keep working forward and to their own right until they were directly behind the Guaranis who were moving away from them.

Mackey, Woods, Koches, Stewart, and O'Connor each took out a grenade and pulled the pin, then ran as fast as they could after the moving army of natives. They threw the grenades as far as they could and dropped to the ground, the five grenades exploding with deafening noise, sending hot shrapnel whizzing through the jungle in all directions. A dozen Guaranis flew through the air, while dozens more dove for cover and tried to figure out what had just happened. They still didn't know that Mackey's crew was behind them, and they cautiously continued moving forward, while Mackey and his men worked their way up quickly behind them.

Mackey opened fire first, in short, silenced bursts. He was joined by his men, who were running, squatting and firing, then moving forward again. They had killed another dozen natives before the Guaranis even knew they were behind them. Once they realized the direction of the fire, the natives spread out and started working their way back towards Mackey's location. In the distance, Mackey could hear Cascaes' unit firing from across the open field.

Stewart was reloading when a Guarani seemed to appear from out of nowhere, brandishing a long club. The warrior, painted red and green, screamed as he flew through the air and swung his weapon at Stewart, who was on one knee changing magazines. Stewart managed to raise his small MP-5 and absorbed the blow, but it knocked him over. The Guarani raised his battle-ax a second time, about to open Stewart's head, when a tremendous blast sent the man flying through the air. Mackey had fired his shotgun and chambered another round as he ran towards Stewart. "Being quiet" was no longer a concern.

Mackey pumped off another three rounds in the general direction of their enemy, and his men continued to fire their machine guns.

Ripper, Cohen and Jones arrived to reinforce Mackey's team, and the Guaranis began disappearing back into the jungle. They reassembled and stopped moving, then Mackey called back to Cascaes. "Jimmy leader, this is Team Two leader. We are reinforced and holding our position. The enemy is retreating."

"Roger that, Team Two. Hold your position," said Cascaes.

Moose, Theresa and McCoy arrived back at Cascaes's location, carrying Santos. As soon as they arrived, Moose looked around and asked where Hodges and Smitty were.

"Hodges is still out on the left flank trying to find something to shoot at—I thought Smitty was with you?" asked Cascaes. He called Smitty on the radio several times but got no answer. The fourth time he was sounding frantic. He popped open his laptop and pulled down the screen to show their locaters. He found Smitty's number at the far edge of their grid, still moving away from them.

"Where the hell is he going?" said Cascaes out loud. He pressed his throat mic. "Hodges—it's Jimmy leader, have you seen Smitty?"

"Negative, Jimmy leader."

Cascaes frowned. "Moose, take Jensen and get back to Hodges. Then the three of you guys see if you can locate Smitty. He is way out there and still moving. Maybe he's running for his life. But stay in touch! I don't want everyone scattered all over the jungle!"

Behind him, Theresa was cutting Santos's pant leg open. The spear was protruding from the front and back of his thigh. She wrapped a pressure bandage around it and popped an IV into his arm. Cascaes knelt down beside her. "Well, doc?"

"This guy's got a spear the diameter of a damn baseball bat through his leg. If I try and pull it out, he'll most likely bleed to death. I don't know how close it is to his femoral artery, and I don't know if I *could* remove it even if I *had* to.

"Well, it's too dangerous to leave him here with only one or two men, and I can't spare more than that. We'll have to take turns carrying him until we take out the village, then we'll all get the hell out of here together."

"If he doesn't bleed to death by then," said Theresa quietly.

"I thought you said he wasn't bleeding badly?" asked Cascaes.

"Yeah, well that was before he was bounced another mile on somebody's back through this jungle."

"Sorry, doc. I don't have a lot of options here. We need to move before they regroup and realize they outnumber us twenty to one." He stood up and checked his weapon. "So much for the element of surprise."

Mackey's shotgun blasting in the background punctuated his sentence.

CHAPTER 33

The Guaranis melted back into the jungle silently, and eventually reached Vega's men, who were holding their position with AK-47s at the ready. Kuka and his warriors passed them by without slowing down, and Vega's men yelled at them to stop running. Kuka had no intention of running away, but rather was finding a better location for ambush. Not speaking much Guarani, Vega's men could only yell obscenities at them and call them cowards as they passed. They hunkered down and waited for the soldiers to approach. Further in the woods to their right, a dozen Guaranis ran through the woods carrying an unconscious soldier, his wrists and ankles bound, bleeding from a head wound. They would be bringing him home, a prize from the battle.

Theresa was pleading her case to Cascaes, about Santos not being moved, when he began convulsing and going into seizures. White foam came out of his mouth, following by waves of vomit as his eyes rolled back in his head.

"Holy shit," screamed Cascaes, "What the hell is wrong with him?"

"Oh my God," yelled Theresa, as she ripped open her bag, looking for a syringe, "It's poison! The fucking Guaranis poisoned the arrows!" She was ripping through her kit, and had pulled out epinephrine just as Santos went limp. "Oh shit—he's crashing!" She popped the epinephrine into his thigh and flipped him on his back, tilting his head, clearing his mouth with her fingers, and started mouth to mouth. Cascaes didn't need an invitation to start CPR as she blew into his mouth. Ernie P. ran over and watched them work on the injured marine.

"Oh shit, doc! What can I do to help?" He pleaded.

She ignored him and kept trying to revive Santos, hoping the epinephrine would relax his airways and tortured blood vessels enough to save him. Cascaes stopped CPR and checked his carotid artery. He had no pulse.

"Don't give up on me, Raul!" he screamed and thumped his chest hard with the bottom of his fist. He started pumping again, Theresa still giving mouth to mouth. They kept at it for another three full minutes, but Santos was completely unresponsive. He was gone. Cascaes stopped first, sitting back on his haunches, looking at the dead body that was Raul Santos. Theresa felt him stop the CPR, and sat up, looking up at Cascaes, tears now starting to come.

"Shit," she said. "Shit, shit, shit!" She punched Santos's still chest. "Fucking poison—I should have assumed they would use it. I should have given him epinephrine as soon as I got to him."

Cascaes looked at her and put his hand on her shoulder. "No way for you to know. It might not have saved him anyway. But distribute what you have to the men. If you have enough, everybody should get a syringe. Tell the crew—they get hit with an arrow or dart, they pop one of those into their thigh and call out for help. Got it?" She nodded, and started taking out all of the epinephrine injections she had.

"Ernie!" yelled Cascaes. "Get some help and double-bag Santos. We'll get him up in a tree for now to keep the animals off of him. His locator is on. We'll pick him up on the way back. Stay alert."

Cascaes called on his throat mic to Mackey. "Jimmy Leader to Team Two leader, you copy?"

"Roger that," said Mackey quietly, as he scanned the jungle in front of him, his shotgun now fully reloaded.

"Santos is KIA. We are regrouping and moving around the left flank to try and find Smitty. Smitty is missing—you copy?"

"Affirmative Jimmy One. Should we hold position or come back around to you?"

"Advance slowly. Move to your left flank as you advance until you join up with us. Alert your team that they will be rejoining us and to check their fire. Over."

"Understood Jimmy One, out."

Cascaes reorganized his team, said a quick goodbye to Santos, and then began moving quickly to their left flank. They came up behind Hodges, who was still scanning across the field with powerful binoculars. He saw the team approaching.

"Skipper, I got nothing. I think they boogied outta' here."

Cascaes nodded and updated Hodges about Santos's death.

"Where are Moose and Jensen? I sent them up here to find Smitty with you?"

"They just checked in, they're doubling back. The jungle got thick as shit out there and they were afraid they were getting lost. They should be back here in a minute. I've just been eyeballing the area across the clearing, hoping maybe I'd spot Smitty, if not the Guaranis." Hodges quickly broke down the bi-pod and stowed his binoculars, and jumped in behind Cascaes' team as they moved out.

With Santos and Smitty both gone from Team One, it ceased to exist. Only Hodges the sharpshooter and McCoy were left from the original four, and they simply rejoined the main group. Team Two, under Mackey, was ahead and to the far right, with almost half of their manpower. Cascaes and his team continued along the edge of the clearing arriving at the scene of the dozens of large spears sticking out of the ground like the back of a porcupine. Theresa had passed out epinephrine to each man and told them to pop one if they got hit by any Guarani projectiles. Seeing the spears in the ground where Santos had gotten hit was a visual reminder. It was there that Moose and Jensen rejoined the group, shaking their heads about not having any luck with Smitty.

Ten minutes of quiet movements through the woods brought them to the center of the opposite side of the clearing. The dead Guarani archer squad leader was their landmark. Hodges saw him and remembered his face through his scope.

"That's for Santos, muthafucker," he said quietly.

Cascaes' earpiece whispered—it was Mackey. "Chris—I've got you dead ahead about a hundred yards. Watch your left flank. They fell back in that direction and should be closer to *you* than *us*. We are moving in your direction slowly."

Cascaes motioned his men to stop and spread out, and they went low and quiet, fanning out in the thick jungle. Birds and monkeys began chattering again, now that the gunfire had stopped. Julia and Theresa stayed close to Cascaes in the center of the team as McCoy, Moose and Jensen worked their way forward and to the left. Hodges began scanning with his sniper scope for any movement.

After a few tense moments, Mackey advised that they were coming in, and to hold fire. The two teams rejoined each other and Mackey and Cascaes caught each other up quickly. Mackey reported on the large number of Guaranis, and confirmed at least twenty kills. He estimated at least twice that number had retreated. There had been no automatic weapon fire, so perhaps Vega's men were guarding the camp.

"The element of surprise is gone," said Cascaes. "We'll keep moving this way and try and track them as we follow Smitty by computer. I don't know if he's running away from them or after them, but we can't leave him lost out here. He seems to be going the same general direction we are, so we can try and keep up with him at the same time that we try and locate their base. I'd still rather get into position near their village and go in at night."

"Absolutely," said Mackey. "They won't have night viz, and the natives won't be as happy about coming out to attack."

"Okay, then let's just keep moving forward, due north, and hope we can pick up their trail. Theresa's got epinephrine syringes for you and your men. Pass them out and tell them the arrows are poisonous—that's what killed Santos. If they get hit with anything, tell them to pop a syringe and call out for the medic."

Mackey was moving towards Theresa when all hell broke out on the left flank. The sound of AK-47s firing long bursts filled the jungle, sent birds up in great clouds.

Moose called in over his mic. "Skipper! We have contact, unknown number at this time, but we are pinned, over!"

"God damn it," said Cascaes. It hadn't been a good day. "Advance! Everyone move up!" The team moved faster through the jungle towards the left flank and sounds of gunfire. Moose, McCoy, and Jensen were returning gunfire in short muffled bursts in the background.

Cascaes and Mackey were running forward and to their right, trying to get behind the sound of the AK-47s, with Ernie P right behind him. An explosion to their far left had Cascaes calling back to Moose on his throat mic. "Moose! What's your situation?"

"That was us. We just cooked a couple of Vega's men. They're falling back and we're moving up. Over"

"Roger that, we are working up to the right," replied Cascaes.

By the time Cascaes and his men linked up with Moose, McCoy and Jensen, the jungle was quiet again. Moose had managed a grenade with his pitcher's arm from a pretty good distance, and had killed three of Vega's men. The rest retreated; Moose was guessing another two or three men at most. Mackey snapped pictures of Vega's men, which he sent via burst transmission back to Langley in case they were valuable targets. The men reloaded, checked weapons, and spread out in a slight "V" with Ripper on point in the center and Moose right behind him. They moved as silently as possible, following the occasional boot prints that they hoped would lead them to Smitty or the village, or maybe both.

A few quiet moments passed, and the jungle was still. The men moved like ghosts through the jungle, not knowing if their enemy was miles away, or behind the next tree. Cascaes whispered into his throat mic to stop, and the men took a knee in the soft jungle floor. Cascaes opened his small computer and scanned for Smitty. The locator was still working, showing Smitty due south, straight ahead of them, but almost a mile out and still moving.

Using Smitty as their new bearing, Cascaes signaled the men to move out again, and they silently worked through the jungle. Julia had come up behind Cascaes when he was using the computer and gave him a smile, but no one was feeling romantic—just sad, angry and stressed. He patted her thigh, a sort of "mini-hug," and then hustled up ahead with Moose and Ripper. They had traveled less than half a mile when the jungle floor began dropping. They found themselves walking down an incline which was becoming steeper. And the ground grew wetter. The vegetation began to change as the earth became swampier. And then they heard it—the sound of running water.

Cascaes sent Moose and Ripper scouting ahead and the rest of the team spread out and checked all directions for movement. Moose and Ripper were gone less than ten minutes.

"White water ahead, Skipper. We found a place to cross, maybe twenty yards across some open rocks. There's a waterfall up ahead to the left, which is the direction of the water flow. Beautiful spot, but maybe beautiful for an ambush. When we cross, we'll be out in the open," reported Moose.

Cascaes checked his watch. It was only fifteen hundred hours, and they couldn't wait for the sun to set. "Okay, we go now. You lead the way."

The team reassembled and followed Ripper single file, with the exception of Moose on the far right and Jones on the far left protecting their flanks. As they walked, the jungle floor became rockier leading to the huge boulders at the stream. The team worked their way through the rocks, and Hodges found a spot to set up his sniper rifle. He would try and cover the crossing from the top of a large boulder, where he relocated a large lizard that had been sunning itself.

Earl Jones and Lance Woods would be crossing the stream first, and they worked their way down the rocks to the edge of the rushing water. The water was moving fast in most parts, crashing over the rocks until it came to a cliff another fifty yards downstream, then tumbled a hundred feet in a dramatic waterfall. Jones and Woods weren't sightseeing. They moved a few feet at a time until they were at the narrowest part of the stream, where rocks protruded from the water enough to run across them without getting wet.

Hodges called on his radio that he couldn't see any movement across the stream, and the two men ran across as fast as they could. The dozens of painted warriors on the far side hid quietly, waiting for the larger group to make their move.

CHAPTER 34

Stream Crossing

Jones and Woods had crouched in the rocks for what seemed like eternity, until Hodges confirmed that it was clear. They readied their MP-5's and ran across the rocks to the far side of the stream. Once there, they took a knee and scanned the woods around them. Woods made a sour face to Jones—something was wrong. One of the things that they had been taught back in Langley by the jungle warfare expert was how to use clues from the jungle to enhance your sense of surroundings. The jungle should have been louder—instead it was still and without sound. The birds and monkeys made no noise, and it wasn't because of Woods and Jones scaring them, or they would have seen the birds take off.

Woods spoke softly into his throat mic. "Skipper, I don't like this."

Cascaes was watching through his binoculars across the stream. "Hodges, you see anything?"

"Negative, Skipper, I..." his voice trailed off. "Woods, check your three o'clock."

Woods crouched lower and looked to his left. He could sense them more than see them. They were amazing people, the way they could disappear into the jungle. But he did see *something*. Very slowly, Woods pulled a grenade from his thigh pocket. Jones watched him and did the same thing, although he hadn't seen anything yet. They both pulled the pins and Woods lobbed his about twenty yards. Jones threw his a few feet to the right,

155

figuring the spot must be where Woods saw something. They both went prone and covered up as the explosions rocked the jungle.

As soon as the grenades went off, Cascaes and his men charged across the stream, with Hodges firing at anything that moved from his location on top of the rock. Vega's three remaining men began firing their AK-47s at Woods and Jones, who returned fire in short bursts. Cascaes and his team spread out as they came up from the rear, and began suppressing fire in the direction of Vega's men. Kuka's warriors attacked in a frontal assault, which was pointless. They never got close to Jones or Woods, who poured machine gun fire into them, reinforced now with the rest of the team. Jon Cohen used his grenade launcher with deadly accuracy, sending Vega's men and dozens of Guaranis flying.

Within moments, it was over. The Guaranis had melted back into the jungle and Cascaes and his men fanned out and secured the area. They found three of Vega's men dead, as well as twenty-eight Guaranis. None of the team was injured. Cascaes opened his computer and looked for Smitty's signal. It was still ahead of them, and still moving away from them.

"Damn," he mumbled and called over to Mackey who took a knee next to him. "I think they've got him, Mack. Smitty's signal is always in the middle of the shit. I think they've taken him prisoner."

Mackey rubbed his chin and grimaced. "Then we better keep pushing, Chris. If you're right, we need to get to him fast. I can't imagine what they'll do to him if we can't get to him in time."

Cascaes nodded and closed his computer, then signaled Ripper to take point. They fanned out a little and moved cautiously after the retreating Guaranis, stopping only once so Cascaes could photograph Vega's three men and send the pictures back to Langley. It was stressful following the Guaranis for hours on end. Every shadow, every bird call or monkey screech made the men pause and look around, weapons at the ready—but they pressed on. One of their own was somewhere ahead of them, along with Vega and his village, and maybe if they were really lucky, a few terrorists as a bonus. They stayed focused and moved ahead.

⊕

Vega was walking to his cabin, AK-47 in hand, when Kuka and some of his warriors began streaming back into the village at a slow run. Vega walked in their direction, pleased at first, especially when he saw them carrying a prisoner suspended from a pole between four Guaranis like a bagged game animal. He looked for his own men and didn't see them. He called to Kuka, who did not look pleased.

"Kuka! What happened? Where is everyone?" screamed Vega as he approached them.

The chief barked back at Vega. "Your men are dead! My warriors are dead! There were too many of them."

Vega had to process the information for a moment. "Wait a minute, Kuka, what are you saying? Did you lead the soldiers back to the village? What did you do? How many of them are there?"

Kuka ignored him and continued to the center of the village where he began screaming at his people. The drums began and the Guarani people descended on their chief from everywhere. He began ranting and screaming at his people, as Vega tried to listen and understand what he was saying. The Guaranis took off in a dozen different directions to gather their belongings. They were leaving.

"Kuka! What are you doing?" demanded Vega.

Raman Qasim, Ali Aziz and Hakim Bin-Salaam appeared, walking towards the center of the village to see what was happening.

"Señor Vega, what is going on?" asked Raman.

Vega ignored the question and kept screaming at Kuka. "What are you doing? You can't leave! Did you lead these soldiers right to me? Kuka?" He approached the chief and was about to grab him by the arm when Kuka turned and began screaming at Vega, waving his spear in Vega's direction. He screamed that it was Vega's fault his warriors were dead, and he was taking his people and leaving.

"Señor Vega!" screamed Raman again, this time a little frantic.

Vega screamed at Raman, "Not now!" and turned back to Kuka. "How many of them are there?"

Kuka ignored him and walked away, sending Vega over the edge. Vega ran to the prisoner who was barely conscious, hanging from his bound wrists and ankles under a pole carried on the shoulders of four of Kuka's men. Vega slapped the man's face repeatedly and screamed at him first in Spanish, then in English. "You American? How many of you are there? How many?"

Smitty looked at the man through swollen eyes and managed a smile. His mouth was dry and caked with his blood. He had taken several blows to the head when he was originally attacked in the jungle right after Santos was speared. He spoke through swollen lips. "Enough to kick your ass, mutherfucker," he said hoarsely. He tried to spit, but his mouth was too dry and his lips were too swollen. One of Kuka's men, who didn't understand the insult, but didn't like Smitty's apparent boldness, pushed a knife into Smitty's tricep and withdrew it slowly. He pushed his finger into the bleeding hole up to his second knuckle, causing Smitty to scream, then withdrew it and sucked the blood off of his finger, all the while smiling at the prisoner. It was apparently a hint of what was to come later. Smitty howled and hung helplessly. Vega was disgusted, but ignored it and asked him again.

"How many of you are there? Tell me and I'll kill you quickly. Tell me!" he screamed. "Or I'll watch these savages peel your skin off and eat you alive!"

Smitty fought back the tears, but remained silent. Vega smashed the prisoner with the butt of his machine gun and kicked the dirt. He was losing it. His remaining men had assembled now with their weapons, and awaited instructions. The three Arabs stood silently, understanding that things were not going very well.

Raman spoke in Arabic to Aziz. Bin-Salaam joined in and the three of them were apparently arguing when Vega told them to shut up. That didn't go over well with Raman Qasim. He barked at Vega, "Señor Vega, we are leaving. You don't have control over this situation. Get us a few guides to lead us back to the river. We want to leave immediately."

Vega laughed like a lunatic. "Oh you think so? You are just going to leave? Well good luck finding the river! Your guides are *leaving*! Do you get it? Kuka and his people are leaving! They have led these fucking commandos right to us, and now they are *leaving*! You want to leave, too? Fine—only good luck finding your way to the river without any guides. *These cowards are deserting*!" Vega was borderline hysterical.

The three men began screaming at each other in Arabic, each blaming the other for their present situation. Kuka reappeared outside his oga, followed by his wives and children, each carrying bundles of family belongings. The drumming began again, as Kuka assembled his people for their journey deeper into the jungle.

CHAPTER 35

The Village

Cascaes and Mackey had been right behind Ripper, who was on point, for over an hour. They were moving at almost a jog, following the signal from Smitty's transponder. When they heard the faint sound of drums, they increased their pace and honed in on the sound. It had to be the village. As the drums grew louder, the signal grew stronger and closer, and the team fanned out. Cascaes fell back and grabbed Julia by the arm, whispering into her ear, "The shit is going to hit the fan in a little bit. You stay close to me and keep low. If I need to go into the village, you stay hidden and keep your eyes open. I assume you know how to use this?" He asked, pointing to the MP-5 she carried.

"I shoot better than you, so just worry about yourself," she said. She didn't want him distracted worrying about her, although she was terrified for the first time in many years. While she had been on countless hairy missions herself, it wasn't the same as actual combat, and what she had seen today would stay with her for a long time.

"Theresa—stay close to Julia," said Cascaes.

"Listen you sexist pig," said Theresa, half serious, "I put marines back together for two years while ragheads tried to blow my head off, so you just worry about your own ass and stop fretting over us women-folk. This is nothing compared to Fallujah."

160

He grunted and trotted ahead after Mackey, who had stopped. Mackey used hand signals for everyone to stop and get low. Ripper called in quietly over his mic.

"I have the village, Skipper, dead ahead. Lots of activity from what I can see. There are a shitload of them, too. Not just men, either, I see women and little kids running around."

"Any sign of Smitty?" asked Cascaes, who inched forward towards Ripper's position. He had his laptop open as he crawled. "He should be ahead of you and to your right. He isn't moving right now."

"I can't see, Skipper. But there are some big-ass houses or something down there. And it looks like the villagers are getting ready to split. They're all carrying stuff. You better take a look."

Cascaes continued to move forward, followed by Mackey and the rest of the team. When he reached Ripper, he crawled over him and took out his binoculars. He scanned the village like Ripper.

"I think you're right, Vinny. They look like they're leaving. Shit. There's tons of non-combatants mixed in with them now. Hey! Jackpot!"

Mackey was behind him. "What have you got?" he asked.

"Vega. Sonofabitch. That's him. He's yelling at, *holy shit*. That's the whole package—Raman Qasim, Aziz, and Bin-Salaam! They're *all* down there!"

"Jackpot is right," said Mackey quietly. "But attacking a couple of hundred villagers wasn't part of the plan. Now what?"

Cascaes bit his lip. "We wait and watch. Shit. No sign of Smitty yet, but they must have him. The signal is coming from the village." He looked at his watch. It was almost eighteen-hundred hours. "Might be another couple of hours of daylight. You think the Guaranis will take off this late in the day? Won't give them much time to set up a new village."

"They might not need much time," answered Mackey, as he watched the Guarani women start to take apart the ogas, plank by plank. "Looks like pre-fab construction."

A scream filled the jungle so gut-wrenching that all activity stopped for a moment.

"Oh, God," said Mackey. "That's Smitty."

"Fuck," said Cascaes with a grunt. "Change of plans. We need to get to him *now*. I'll take half of the team and circle around to the right. Hodges, you find a spot that gives you some targets and cover us when we move in. Mackey, move forward and start shooting when I signal you. Maybe you can distract them enough that we can get in and grab Smitty. Hodges, if you can find the four primary targets when the shooting starts, you are cleared to fire, understand?"

"Roger that, Skipper, it'll be my pleasure." Hodges moved silently ahead and to the left looking for a place that would give him a better view. He looked up at the giant twisted tree overhead and smiled, adjusting the rifle on his back as he began quietly climbing.

Cascaes signaled for Moose, Ripper, McCoy, Cohen and Koches to follow him. Everyone else stayed with Mackey and started inching forward towards the village, as Hodges settled into a large branch twenty feet off the ground and began adjusting his scope. From the village, Smitty's uncontrolled screaming filled the jungle.

Hodges called in to Cascaes that he could see Smitty. Vega and a few Guaranis were poking and cutting him, and he asked for permission to take them out. Cascaes told him to wait— Smitty would have to tough it out a few more minutes until Cascaes and his men were closer. If he fired too soon, they were all screwed. Hodges kept his sight on the back of Vega's head, dying inside as he watched the animal torturing his friend. Cascaes and his team moved as quickly as they could, circling around to the right, as Mackey's team fanned out at the edge of the village clearing and took up firing positions. As soon as they got the command, they would begin assaulting and causing as much damage as possible, allowing Cascaes and his team to come from the rear. Jones had a grenade launcher at the ready, but was tentative as he watched the children mixed in with the adults.

Mackey saw his face and called over to him quietly. "That's Smitty out there screaming, Earl. If you can't fire that weapon when I tell you, then give it to someone who can."

"I'm cool," replied Jones quietly, as he inched forward through the thick underbrush.

The next few minutes seemed to take forever as Cascaes and his team moved into position. Smitty was screaming when Cascaes radioed back to Mackey.

"Okay Mac, we're in position, about thirty yards from Smitty. Come heavy and grab their attention, and we'll try and grab him. I can see Vega, but don't have a clear shot. Hodges, can you see the other three targets?"

"Affirmative, skipper," said Hodges from up in the giant tree. "I don't have great shots on them either because of all the damn villagers, but I'll do what I can."

"Okay, Mac, on three you turn this place upside down, and Hodges you start taking out your targets. One...two...*three!*"

Mackey and his men opened fire simultaneously and moved towards the village in an all-out assault. Hodges fired his first shot which almost decapitated Ali Aziz. His white beard was now full of blood and brain matter as he fell like a stone to the ground. As chaos ensued in the following moments, with villagers screaming and running in all directions, Cascaes and his team sprinted from the tree line into the village, firing short deliberate bursts at the men around Smitty, who dropped to the ground. Vega turned and ran, after throwing a Guarani in the direction of the gunfire to shield himself. He disappeared into the crowd of screaming villagers as they all took off in every direction.

Cascaes, Moose, Ripper, McCoy, Cohen, and Koches advanced, firing and reloading magazines as fast as they could. Smitty was on the ground only semi-conscious, still tied to the long pole, bleeding from dozens of wounds. Several Guaranis were dead on the ground around him. Moose was the first to get to him, and used his Ka-Bar knife to quickly cut him loose. He threw Smitty over his shoulder and ran back into the forest with the rest of the team slowly backing up while firing to cover his escape.

The Guaranis were not fighting back; they were running for their lives. Women picked up small children and babies and ran full speed, screaming in panic. Kuka had disappeared into the jungle, followed by dozens of his people. They had been caught completely off guard, not realizing that the soldiers could possibly track them so quickly. Vega had disappeared along with him, and Hodges had only been able to hit Aziz. Hakim Bin-Salaam and Raman Qasim had both hit the dirt and scrambled through the villagers to avoid giving Hodges a clear shot, and after the truck incident back in Saudi Arabia, Hodges couldn't pull the trigger with women and children running all over the place.

Mackey and his men continued firing, and Jones managed to fire half a dozen grenades at small groups of warriors that attempted to get organized. It was five minutes of loud gunfire and explosions, and then total silence. Cascaes and his men rejoined Mackey, with Smitty still out of it on Moose's back. Theresa came running and checked his pulse. Being unsure whether or not they had poisoned him, she hit him with a shot of epinephrine, which woke him up. He was bleeding from a dozen minor wounds to his arms and legs, but the Guaranis had been interrupted before the serious hacking had started. Theresa gave him half a syringe of morphine, enough to kill some of the pain, but not put him out totally—they needed him on his feet. She dressed his wounds quickly, impressing the men with her speed and quality of work. Smitty clenched his teeth and waited for the morphine to kick in. It was obvious she was very experienced.

Mackey and Cascaes looked at each other. Mackey spoke first. "Well, this is a clusterfuck. Vega is in the wind and Hodges only got Aziz. Now what?"

Cascaes looked at Smitty and gently slapped his face. "Hey, Smitty! How you feeling, baby? You ready to run through the jungle?"

Theresa looked at him, shaking her head.

"I'm okay, skipper. Thanks for coming to get me, I thought they were gonna' make soup out of me, man." His speech was slurred slightly, but he was coherent. Cascaes and Moose helped him up. He could stand, but just barely. Moose looked at him and then at Cascaes. "He'll be okay. Little fucker doesn't weight too much. We'll keep up. Won't we, Pin-cushion Boy"

Smitty tried his best to act tough through his pounding headache. "Roger that, Moose-Man."

Cascaes grunted. "Good man. Okay, then. Everyone reload, hydrate, and get ready to move out."

Moose and Ripper held Smitty and made him drink some water, then poured some on his head and wiped off his face. He looked like Hell, but he was a tough little dude and tried his best to shake off the morphine and the pain. He had bandages all over his arms and legs and he was wrapped around his head, making him look like a car accident victim out of a bad movie.

Moose leaned close to his ear and whispered, "Listen Smitty, we need to bungle through the jungle—you just hang on to ol' Moose and let me do the work, ya' hear? I'll carry you if you feel funky, you just tell me. But we need to hustle, so don't be proud, okay?"

Smitty leaned over and vomited up the water he had just drank, then looked up at Moose and tried a weak smile. "I ain't feelin' too proud, brother. I'll be hanging on tight."

Moose gave him his canteen and told him to swish and spit, then take a few baby sips. Cascaes and Mackey had conferred and rejoined the group which assembled around them in a small huddle, locked and loaded.

Cascaes spoke up, "Okay, here it is—we have Vega, Bin-Salaam and Raman Qasim on the run in the jungle. We have no idea where they are headed because they probably have no idea where they are headed. There are a couple of hundred Guaranis running around out there with them, armed with poison darts, spears and maybe a few AK-47s. We are going to stay together and follow the general direction of their retreat out the back of the village and try and pick up their trail. It will start getting dark in a few hours. We're hoping the Guaranis pick a spot and settle down for the night. With our night vision, maybe we can get lucky and pick up our three targets running through the jungle. Hopefully, they'll be the only ones moving after dark. We will move forward in a forty yard spread. Make sure you can maintain a constant visual on the people next to you. Ripper, you are far right flank and Cohen, you are far left. Jones, you still have thumper—how many grenades do you have left?"

"Six," he replied.

"Anybody else have any?" asked Cascaes.

Moose and McCoy each flipped him three more, which he shoved into his oversized cargo pants pockets.

"Recheck comm. Equipment and night viz right now, then fan out and get ready to boogie."

Each person checked their throat mics and earpieces, then turned the night vision on and off to make sure it was operational. All was well. They spread out, with Cascaes and Mackey next to each other in the center, and Theresa and Julia a few paces behind them. The rest of the team was spread out along a forty yard front and began moving quickly and quietly through the jungle.

CHAPTER 36

The trail wasn't hard to follow, for a change. While the warriors were truly invisible in the jungle, a couple of hundred panic stricken women and children were not. Hundreds of footprints and broken vegetation made their exit from the village easy to follow for the first half mile. As the Guaranis calmed down, they began moving more carefully, and the trail became slightly harder to follow, but still, a few hundred people left signs in the fragile jungle.

The team maintained silence for almost two hours, each person in total concentration of their surroundings. Each person would constantly check the person on his right or left, and use hand signals only, but focused on following as quickly as possible. As the sun started to drop behind the jungle canopy, the shadows of the jungle made the trail more difficult to follow. Cascaes quietly told his team to halve the size of their intervals, so they'd be closer together. They took a five minute break for water, a power bar and a pee, then broke out their night vision equipment. It was still too bright out to use it, but at least they'd be ready.

Another thirty minutes of following the trail through the thick brush went quickly, and then all of them sensed it simultaneously. The jungle had gotten very still. Cascaes signaled a halt, and they all crouched in the thick underbrush. Was it just the setting sun that had the animals settling down for the night, or was it the natives scaring them off? Cascaes signaled Woods and Koches to scout ahead. They were both army rangers and very comfortable in the jungle. In fact, Koches had eaten some of the caterpillars that Fuzzy had eaten earlier just to gross out his squad mates. It had worked.

The two of them moved slowly ahead of the group until they disappeared into the thick vegetation. Theresa used the down time to change some of Smitty's bandages and pop an IV into his arm to make sure he was hydrated. Within five minutes of the IV drip, his color got much better and his eyes started to clear for the first time. Moose knelt next to him, holding up the drip bag like Poppa Bear protecting a cub. Moose had pretty much carried Smitty with one arm for most of the evening, but looked no worse for wear.

It started getting dark and Mackey's nerves finally got to him. He spoke into his mic, "Jimmy to point, sit-rep, over."

There was a few seconds before a very quiet whisper came back from Koches.

"Point is in the middle of Guarani central. Looks like they are making some kind of shelters. They're all huddling up. Hard to see much, it's really thick out here. No sign of our three primary targets yet. Still scouting, out."

It was obvious they didn't want to keep speaking from their location, so Mackey bit his bottom lip and tried to be patient. Cascaes whispered for him to "be cool" and took out an MRE, which he held up for everyone to see. It was the dinner bell. Everyone took out their foil packs and tore them open, adding water from their canteens to enjoy the delicious freeze dried dinners they would try and choke down. Cascaes mixed up his pack and then crawled over to Julia and handed it to her.

"You only bring me to the finest places," she said.

"Yeah, the service is better than the food though," he said with a smile.

"Well I wouldn't know about your service, would I?" she said, dramatically batting her eyelashes. Even though she was joking, it still gave Cascaes a pang. She was beautiful, even covered with grimy grease paint and dozens of cuts and bruises. He considered a comeback, but opted not to speak. He just broke out another MRE and added some water for himself. Julia smiled at him, a genuine smile from her heart. She was partly laughing at herself. After being around hundreds of guys who fought for her attention, how was it possible that she found herself falling for a guy in the middle of a sweaty jungle during a small war.

She "clinked" his foil bag with hers, as if to say "cheers," and whispered, "Our first dinner date. How romantic." They were somewhat lost in each others' gaze when Koches's voice broke up their little dinner party.

"Jimmy, this is point. There is zero movement out here right now. It's like with Fuzzy, these people don't like the dark. They made little shelters out of wood bark and leaves and some of the stuff from the village, and they are all piled up together in little groups. There was something big going on a few minutes ago about a hundred yards ahead of me, beyond the Guaranis, but I couldn't see anything from here. Some kind of commotion, then nothing. When it gets darker, I'll move around the villagers and take a look."

"Negative, point. Hold your position. I am tracking your location by computer and we will move up to you. When it gets darker, we'll take a look. Sit tight," said Cascaes.

Koches and Woods moved a few yards back into the jungle, thirty yards from where the Guaranis had settled into their night encampment. They lay on their stomachs, weapons in front of them at the ready, and tried to relax and wait.

Fifteen minutes later, the rest of the team arrived, belly crawling up from behind them. Cascaes stopped right at Koches's elbow. Koches pointed to some piles of leaves and wood that blended into the jungle floor and underbrush. As if by magic, a couple of hundred people had simply disappeared into the jungle floor. It was now dark enough to pop on their night vision goggles, and in the bright green world in front of them, they could easily make out Guarani women nursing babies under the sticks and leaves that made their temporary home. Men sat with spears across their laps and children sleeping behind them.

Cascaes whispered to Koches, "I wish all of our enemies were scared of the dark."

Following Cascaes and Koches, the team moved single file, extremely slowly around the makeshift camp. No one made a sound, but kept close watch on the figures they could make out in the dark. Koches led to where he had heard the commotion earlier, somewhat guessing at the exact location. He was the first to see it. He couldn't help an audible "holy shit."

Enrique Antonio Vega had caused trouble for Kuka for the last time. His body was hanging between two large poles that had been thrust through his armpits and out his shoulders, and he had been stripped of his clothes. The Guaranis had skinned his chest and stomach, presumably while he was alive, and pulled out some of his intestines. His face was frozen in a silent scream, his mouth propped open with small sticks—his tongue having been removed. Blood must have been pouring out from his mouth and exposed body, as it covered him and the plants beneath him, now festering with bugs eager to have a late supper. Only the top portion of Vega's face was without blood, and his eyes were wide open, frozen in his final second of terror. There was no way for Koches to know as he looked at the mutilated corpse, that a young Guarani girl had been the one to hack off his genitals as payback for his abuses.

Koches was no lightweight, and thought he had seen it all over his twelve years in the rangers, including a stint in Somalia, but he almost vomited. Cascaes saw it a few seconds after him and felt a similar retching in his stomach.

"Couldn't have happened to a nicer guy," he whispered to Koches. He took out his tiny computer, which had a built-in camera, and snapped a few pictures of Vega. He typed out a quick message: *Primary target found. Guaranis beat us to him.* He hit send and the burst transmission was encrypted and bounced off a satellite to Langley.

Mackey came up slowly and whispered to Cascaes. "We call this a success and get the hell out of here, or you think we have a shot at getting the other two?"

Cascaes thought for a second. "I think Smitty is keeping up just fine. Let's keep moving in this direction and see if we can catch up to the other two jokers. My guess is, they are terrified, assuming they are still alive, and must be running like hell through the jungle. If so, they'll leave an easy trail and we'll find them tonight or tomorrow morning. If we don't catch up to them by tomorrow afternoon, we'll let the jungle or the Guaranis have them and start working on our extraction plan. According to the map, we should hit a river up ahead in about three miles. The current will bring us back out of the jungle and save a day of travel time."

"We don't have the boats," said Mackey, thinking about Piranhas and alligators.

"We're SEALs, Mac. We always have a way to work the water—don't get yourself all worked up," he said with a smile. "Don't worry; I won't let anything eat you."

Julia worked her way up to Cascaes. She had already gotten an eyeful of Vega hanging between the poles. "Hey," she whispered. "I have an idea."

"Shoot," said Cascaes.

"You know, the reason the Guaranis are afraid of the dark if because they are animists. They believe in the animal spirits that come out at night. Let's fuck with them." She said it with anger in her voice.

"Say what?" asked Cascaes.

"They killed one of your men, almost killed another, and you can see what they'll do to all of us if they catch us," she said, pointing to Vega's festering corpse. "They are *scared* of the animal spirits. Let's give them something to be scared of."

Without waiting for permission, she knelt in the direction of the Guaranis, cupped her hands around her mouth, and let out a long "*arrrrrroooooooooooooooo!*"

Cascaes and Mackey were shocked. "Are you fucking insane?" asked Cascaes, "why don't you just tell them where we are while you're at it!"

"No, no!" said Mackey, "She's right. Look at their little shelters, they're pulling them as tightly closed as they can!" Mackey scrambled through the underbrush, closer to the natives and let out a blood-curdling howl. He spoke into his throat mic and called to the entire team. "These fuckers are scared of the animal spirits! Give them something to have nightmares about!"

The entire team was up in an instant, running through their makeshift shelters, howling like monkeys, coyotes or just outright screaming. It was actually very cathartic for the team that had been in combat mode for so long. They were up and running like lunatics, their night vision equipment giving them perfect glimpses of the terrified Guaranis huddled under their giant leaves and pieces of wood. The longer it went on, the bolder they got, running closer to the shelters, even smacking them as they screamed and howled, trying their best to sound terrifying. The adrenaline and borderline hysteria fed upon itself, and before long, every member of the team, including Smitty, was up and running around the shelters. For the terrified Guaranis, all they could see were the bright green eyes of the phantom animals that glowed in the dark. They huddled close, spears at the ready—but they were not feeling like warriors anymore, they were simply terrified children living a nightmare.

When the team had run out of adrenaline, they reassembled on the back side of the camp by Vega's body. They smiled as they heard children crying from the small shelters. Smitty quietly said, "Fuck you" to the sobbing as he touched his pounding arm. "I hope you have nightmares for a year," he

THE TEAM BOOK II: INTO THE JUNGLE

said quietly. The team fanned out and began moving away from the Guaranis, trying to pick up the trail of their last two targets. Jones was the one who found the footprints.

"Skipper! I got boot prints!" he called in from the left flank. The team moved to his location, and sure enough, the boot prints were clearly visible in the mud. Broken plant stems and footprints continued ahead of them, and they reassembled single file behind Jones. Jones, a marine recon scout, was an excellent tracker, and led them through the jungle at a brisk jog. They moved quickly through the cooler jungle, with only occasional bats fluttering overhead. For the most part, the jungle was quiet.

Jones held up a hand and the team stopped. Cascaes moved up behind him.

"What is it?" he asked.

"They must be getting tired. They're walking now. Check out the spacing of their prints. Also—you notice we're drifting right? The slope goes that way. They're tired and moving downhill—I bet they don't even know it. They can't be that much farther ahead of us, Skipper. They can't see at night and it's zero-viz without night vision. They are walking blind up ahead. Are we capturing them or just taking them out?"

That was an interesting question. It had never occurred to them that they could potentially take prisoners. Live terrorists might be worth more than dead ones. It would also be a major pain in the ass getting them out of the jungle and back to an extraction point. "Sit tight," he told Jones.

Cascaes moved back to Mackey. "Hey, Mac. We can probably take these alive at night. They'll never see us coming. What do you think?"

Mackey rubbed his chin. "Shit."

"Yeah, that's what I thought, too."

"Let's make a phone call," he said. They signaled for everyone to take five, and the team dropped to a knee and made a quick perimeter. Mackey and Cascaes opened up a satellite phone and unfolded a small dish that they gave to Hodges, who uncoiled some wire and climbed a tree to get some clearance.

Mackey dialed the secure number for Darren Davis's portable emergency phone and waited. The conversation would be sent via small burst transmissions that were encrypted, bounced off a satellite, and then unscrambled at the other end. It made the voices tinny and created gaps between speakers, but at least they could call direct from anywhere in the world.

Thousands of miles away, Darren Davis was having dinner at his desk in Langley. It was bad Chinese take-out, but in a pinch, it *was* food. When his emergency phone turned red and buzzed, he almost spit out his bok choy.

"Wolf here," he said into the small phone.

After a brief pause, he could hear Mackey's voice. "This is Jimmy leader with a sit-rep. We have one KIA and one minor wounded, but have eliminated one target and found the other dead. Powder (the code name for Vega), is very much dead, and so is Rag Two (Code name for Aziz). Picture should be in your computer. Rag One and Rag Three (Raman Qasim and Hakim Bin-Salaam), are on the run. We may be able to take them home gift-wrapped. You want to open the present at home, or should we just open it here and leave it?"

Davis was a little taken back on his end. He processed the information as fast as possible, then responded.

"Jimmy leader, I am sorry to hear about your team member. I need his jersey number. If you can bring me two souvenirs from your trip without compromising your safety, I'd love to open those presents. But only if you can bring them home without any problems. First sign of trouble, you throw them away, understand?"

"Understood. Number nine on the roster is gone. We will try and bring him home on the way out if possible. We will attempt to grab you the souvenirs and expect a two-day trip to an extraction location. Will we have a taxi waiting?"

"We will need to work out some details if you have two packages. Advise me as soon as you can. Good luck."

"Okay, we'll be in touch, most likely before first light. Over and out."

The phone and dish were disassembled in seconds and the team moved out after Jones. Several of the team members had turned off the night vision to get a taste of the jungle without their goggles, and they couldn't see their hands in front of their faces. There was no moon, but even if it had been out, the double canopy of the jungle was much too thick to let in any light anyway.

They moved quickly through the jungle, following the footprints. It was evident from the occasional handprints and flattened undergrowth that the men they were chasing were stumbling and falling. Jones smiled as he moved. "We're coming mutherfuckers," he said to himself, then sang his best Jimi Hendrix impersonation. "Here I come, baby...comin' to getcha'..."

CHAPTER 37

Raman Qasim and Hakim Bin-Salaam had seen with their own eyes what the savages did to Enrique Antonio Vega. The once powerful, self-proclaimed king of the jungle had been ripped apart before their very eyes, and it was only the frenzy of hate and anger directed at him that kept them from being next. When Kuka ordered Vega put up on stilts, the warriors were quick to respond and enjoyed every minute of what they considered revenge for the loss of their homes and deaths of some of their people.

It didn't take more than two seconds for the two Arabs to decide it was time to start running for their lives. Although they knew they were already lost in the jungle, they would rather take their chances with animals and starvation than be tortured or eaten by these savages. Qasim was the first to bolt, but Bin-Salaam was hot on his tail. They both ran for almost forty minutes straight, ignoring the stitch in their sides and heaving lungs. Fear was a powerful motivator. What they had witnessed with Vega would keep their legs moving much longer than they had thought possible.

The problem was, they had no idea where they were going. They didn't know what direction they were moving in, and had no idea of their location. They did know it seemed to be further into the jungle, which was obviously not where they wanted to go, but until the sun came out, they just wanted to get as far away from the Guaranis as possible. They were both completely hysterical for the first twenty minutes, awaiting arrows or poison darts that never came as they ran.

After about an hour, their legs and lungs finally started to betray them, and as the adrenaline left them, they found themselves terrified and exhausted. They hadn't eaten much that day because they found everything but the fish and bananas to be disgusting. There hadn't been fish that morning, hence the grumbling in their bellies. Now, it was pitch black and they could be walking in circles for all they knew. At one point, maybe an hour or two earlier, it was hard to judge, they thought they had heard the howling of a pack of animals, and that had increased their pace for a while. Now, however, they were lost, tired and terrified. Bin-Salaam was barely keeping it together. The man who had been responsible for murders all over the globe was now crying like a baby, scared of the dark, and truth be told, of being eaten alive.

Raman Qasim felt his way through the total darkness. He couldn't even see his own hand directly in front of his face. Hakim held his shirt tail and stumbled along behind him, crying and annoying Raman.

"Stop crying like a woman, Hakim!" he finally screamed, "Or I swear I'll leave you here by yourself!" He was bluffing, of course. The idea of being completely alone in the jungle was terrifying; he just needed Hakim to get a grip on himself before Hakim's panic became his own.

"I'm *trying*," he whined. "I can't help it—did you see what they did to Vega? They will eat us if they catch us!"

"Shut up or they *will* catch us!" snapped Raman. "We have to keep moving. Those savages don't like moving at night. We must get as far away as possible before the sun comes up."

"We don't even know where we are going," whined Hakim. "We might be headed straight for them for all we know."

Raman stopped and guessed where Hakim would be behind him, and tried to slap him in the dark. He was only intending to snap him out of his panic, but accidentally popped his nose hard enough to make it bleed and knock him down. As he fell, he still held Raman's shirt and pulled him down with him. The two of them tumbled a few feet into some animal that was startled from its sleep and took off through the underbrush, scaring the shit out of both of them. The hair on their arms was standing up and they both screamed out loud.

A hundred yards behind them, Earl Jones held up his hand and everyone stopped. He whispered into his throat mic.

"I heard something. Up ahead to our right. Slow and easy—advance."

The team fanned out to their right and moved ahead in total silence. When they were close enough to see their two targets, it was all they could do not to laugh. Several peacocks where fluttering around them, having been rousted from their sleep, and the half-dozen birds had evidently terrified the two men who were blind in the dark. One of them was crying out loud and hugging the other one, who was desperately trying to beat him off of him and stand up. The team fanned out around the two of them and watched in silence, completely entertained by these two idiots.

Cascaes was standing there grinning, with Julia next to him holding his arm. Her other hand was over her mouth as she tried not to laugh at the terrified men rolling around with the fluttering birds. Cascaes finally signaled to Moose and Ripper who handed their machine guns to the men next to them and advanced with their knives, still in the sheathes. They didn't want to kill them unless they had to.

Moose and Ripper advanced in complete silence, with Jones and Koches right behind them holding plastic ties that would serve as handcuffs.

Moose and Ripper were able to walk right up on the two men, who finally had managed to separate themselves and start to stand up. It was obvious that they were completely blind in the dark, and the one man was desperately trying to hang on to the other, who was obviously agitated. He was speaking in harsh Arabic to the man as the two of them got to their feet. Moose and Ripper approached them from behind and each placed the tips of their knife sheathes at the base of each man's skull.

"Do not move!" said Moose in a steady firm voice. "I know you speak enough English to know that I will rip your fucking head off and feed it to the Guaranis if you move a fucking muscle."

Each of the Arabs slowly raised their hands. With a heavy accent, the one called Raman said, "Do not shoot."

The other man praised God for being rescued from the Guaranis. He was chattering a hundred miles an hour, obviously thrilled to be captured by Americans. The electric chair was better than another minute in this jungle.

"Shut up!" commanded Ripper, but the man kept praising God. Moose pushed the sheathed knife against Raman's neck. "Tell him to shut up!"

Raman repeated that in Arabic and English, but the man was almost hysterical. "I have been telling him to shut up for two hours," he said in his broken English.

"Tell him if he doesn't shut up, I am going to kill him right now. I mean it," said Moose. And he really *did* mean it.

Raman repeated in Arabic several times, and the man finally stopped his chattering. Jones and Koches grabbed the men by their arms and told them that they would be handcuffed in front of them. They used the heavy duty plastic ties to secure their wrists together, and then used rope to tie the two of them to each other around their waists. Mackey walked up the two of them and grabbed Raman by his shirt.

"Raman Qasim, you are under arrest. We are going to bring you to fair trial and a fair firing squad you piece of shit. Personally, I would much rather just tie you to a tree and leave you here for the animals or the Guaranis to eat, so don't fuck with me. If you try and escape, if you touch any of my people, if you piss me off in any way—I *will* leave you here to die slowly, do you understand me?" He smacked his face hard enough to fill the quiet jungle with the noise.

Raman spit blood and quietly said he understood. "Tell *him*," said Mackey.

Raman repeated it in Arabic to Hakim, who understood most of what had been said, but was not very fluent in English. Cascaes ordered them to sit, which they did, and then gave them water when they asked for it. They set up the phone again, told Darren Davis they had two presents for him, and they would start to figure out a way out of the Godforsaken jungle as fast as possible.

Cascaes checked his map and had the team assembled single file, with the two prisoners in the middle of the line. They headed straight for the river, now only about a mile ahead of them, and walked briskly in total silence.

A few miles away, terrified Guaranis huddled in their tiny shelters, praying for the morning sun to come as fast as possible.

CHAPTER 38

The River

It took forty minutes to travel the one mile to the river. The team only had one extra set of night vision goggles, which had belonged to Santos, and they gave them to the sobbing Hakim to try and calm him down. Raman, still totally blind in the dark, stumbled along, slowing them down. Eventually, Moose had Raman grab hold of his shirt and hang on to him to avoid falling down. Jones, scouting up ahead, called back to the team when he reached the river, and they doubled timed it as best they could with the two prisoners in tow.

The team assembled on the bank of the river. In the dark, it was hard to tell what color the water was, but debris in the water that floated by told of a strong current.

"Okay, listen up. My SEALs, you remember how we got out of that little jam in Africa back in '09? Grab some det cord and get busy! Everybody else, pull your packs apart. We need to travel light and be as invisible on the water as possible. There are mosquito nets with the bedding. Cut them open into large sheets and start jamming leaves and twigs into them to make tarps like giant Ghilly suits. We are going to cover ourselves with it, understand? Camouflage, so get busy."

As he spoke, the SEALs that had served under him for years, Ripper, Moose, Jensen, McCoy, Cohen and O'Conner, had jogged off towards a stand of trees. They wrapped det cord around the base of the trees and attached it to a detonator. "Fire in the hole!" yelled McCoy as he hit the detonator, and the explosion dropped six very large trees.

"Okay, ladies and gentlemen, our chariot awaits! Help get these trees stripped down until the middles are mostly trunk, then we'll lash them together as best we can. Leave some branches and leaves for cover, though. When we have them put together, we will straddle this sucker and cover up with our camo-sheets, understand? We'll use branches and leaves as oars, but the current will mostly move us along. Looks like five to eight knots judging from the debris, so we should make decent time. The river should get faster as we head downstream. Okay, people, *move*! I want to be as far away from these Indians as possible when the sun comes up!"

The team moved quickly, some of them ripping apart the netting and making camouflage out of it as others stripped the trees and then used ropes, bungee cords and vines to try and hold the mess together. The two prisoners sat in the grass helplessly, thanking Allah the merciful that they had been plucked from the hands of the savages. The Americans had rules. A jail cell was nothing compared to being ripped apart and eaten alive.

In less than an hour, the makeshift raft was pushed into the water. The trees sank halfway into the water, and as the team climbed aboard, they sank even further. Mackey whispered to Cascaes, "You sure this thing is gonna float, Chris?"

"I traveled eighty miles on a raft like this once, you're gonna' have to trust me on this one."

"Chris, you guys are part *fish*—you have my *total* trust, believe me."

They pulled the Arabs aboard, placing them again in the center of the raft where they could keep an eye on them. Cascaes was up front, and Julia had nonchalantly managed to get behind him where she could wrap her arms around his waist.

"You think you're riding a motorcycle?" he whispered to her.

"More like a log flume. I'm pretty impressed, Chris," she whispered into his ear.

Moose and Ripper, the team strong-men, pushed the raft into the current, and then climbed on board. As they straddled the raft, they others helped pull what amounted to several large blankets over them. While it didn't cover them completely, unless you were really looking for them, they looked like a bunch of tress that had washed into the river and were simply floating downstream. There were plenty of other debris on the water, and they weren't out of place. Under the tarp, each man had an MP-5 across his lap, except for Hodges, who had his sniper rifle out with his night scope on and a condom over the end of his rifle to keep out any moisture. He babied his rifle, but it was his best friend in the field.

The nineteen of them sat single file straddling the trees, holding branches and trying not to move so the raft wouldn't roll too much. The mosquito nets covered them as much as possible, but it was still pitch black, so it wouldn't matter for a few hours.

Cascaes whispered for the team to try and grab some sleep in intervals, starting with even numbers. He was number one, in the front of the raft.

"Does that mean I get to take a nap?" whispered Julia.

"Sure does," said Chris.

"But you'll still respect me in the morning, right? I mean if we sleep together on only our second date."

"I'm not actually sleeping, so I don't think it counts. Grab some sleep if you can without falling overboard."

She laid her head against his back, her arms around him, thinking about how much she liked this man, and actually managed to fall into a light sleep. The raft moved along silently, without incident for the rest of the night. They were on the Rio Uruguay now, which split off the Rio Parana and headed east towards Brazil before bending south and draining a couple of hundred miles away at the Uruguay – Argentine border. The river continued to get wider and faster, and another float of logs actually caught up to theirs and offered some extra protection. It tangled into theirs, and made their float look even less like a manmade object.

By the time the sun started to break off to their left, most of them had managed at least two hours of sleep. They were soaked from the waist down, and not particularly comfortable, but at least they were away from the Guaranis and headed in the direction of home. Julia lifted her head off of Chris's back and arched and stretched her neck. She let out a small groan as she tried to loosen up. Her arms were still around Chris's waist.

"I think I actually slept," she said to him quietly.

"Julia, you were snoring so loud I thought the Guaranis would find us."

"No way!" she said with a smile, and smacked his thigh playfully.

The team began taking off their night vision equipment and sealing it up in the packs that were acting as pillows and headrests on top of their boat. Orange and pink streaks spread across the morning sky, and birds began to wake up and flutter out of the trees. The morning sounds of the jungle woke up the last of the sleeping crew.

Those that weren't awakened by the birds where awaken by Cascaes.

"Feet out of the water!" he screamed, as he pulled his feet up in front of him on top of the log and grabbed Julia's legs, wrapping them around his waist.

"What's wrong?" asked Julia, taken by surprise.

The fish answered her. A school of piranhas jumped out of the water in front of them, some of them actually sailing across the raft in their excitement.

"Piranhas!" yelled Cascaes, "Feet out of the water!"

The rest of the team began screaming about the piranhas and lifting up their feet. Only Hakim Bin-Salaam, not understanding English so well, was slow to react. As the team members tried to get their own legs repositioned without falling overboard or knocking anyone else over by accident, no one paid attention to the prisoners. At least, that is, until Hakim started screaming. The school of piranhas had been chasing a few larger fish and had begun their usual feeding frenzy when the raft happened to float into them. While the fish were not really after human flesh, Bin Salaam's legs *were* in the water, and his many cuts from the night before put the smell of blood around him. It didn't take long for dozens of hungry, razor sharp tooth-filled mouths to find his lower legs to feed on.

Hakim had no idea what was happening to him, and he panicked. As the school of fish tore into his flesh, he began flailing wildly, almost knocking Raman, who was in front of him, overboard. Raman, who had already had all that he could take of Hakim's hysteria, turned around.

"Get off of me! You are going to knock me off!" he screamed and shoved Hakim with his cuffed hands. Hakim, unable to grab anything with his hands cuffed together, slid off over the side backwards, even as Jones, who was behind him, tried to grab him. Hakim, who couldn't swim very well at all to begin with, and now had his hands cuffed together, disappeared into the brown water. The splashing of hundreds of fish engulfed the raft. Jones, who was going to try and jump in after him, leaned away in horror as the water turned red with blood and dozens of large red bellied piranhas leapt out of the river. Their mouths snapped open and closed, showing the hundreds of teeth as they tried to bite at anything they could find. Theresa, who was sitting behind Jones, starting shrieking, and pulled Jones back towards her so he couldn't go after him. Smitty, who was sitting behind her, put his hand over her eyes and said, "Don't look," as the cloud of killer fish shredded the body in the water.

The raft continued to float, thankfully away from the school of feeding fish. Hakim never broke the surface, to the relief of the horrified onlookers, who were waiting to hear his screaming. Instead, the only noise was the splashing of over-excited fish having their morning feeding.

Jon Cohen, who was sitting in front of Raman, turned around and looked at him with disgust. "That was your buddy, huh? You pussy. That's how you guys look out for each other? You're a fucking coward. I ought to throw you in after him."

Mackey, who was in front of Jon, leaned back and told him to shut up.

Cascaes, half-way turned around, was holding Julia, who had buried her head in his shoulder. "Everybody stay quiet. Keep your feet out of the water for a while. The fish are most active at sunup for their first feeding. Keep your eyes open for gators, too. Not everything that looks like a log *is* a log. Stay sharp and keep your weapons ready. I'm going to try and figure out where the hell we are. Keep an eye on Raman back there, too. I want to bring him back alive, but if he tries anything funny, Jones you slit his fucking throat and throw him to the fish."

"Aye-aye, Skipper. It would be my pleasure," replied Jones

Raman, humiliated, sat crossed legged on the raft, his hands in his lap, aware of the warm urine he was sitting in. Evidently, he had been more terrified than he knew.

CHAPTER 39

Cascaes sat on the world's most primitive raft with one of the world's most sophisticated computers. He was looking at their position on his GPS map. They had traveled over fifty miles since they had gotten on the river the night before. They were far, far away from the Guaranis, who were probably still terrified from the spirits in the night. The river had been swift, and had taken them much further than they had anticipated. They were many miles away and hadn't heard the single gunshot that echoed through the jungle when Carlos, Vega's last surviving man, blew his own brains out in the dark of night.

Cascaes set up the satellite phone with some help from Julia, and called Davis again. Davis answered, sounding groggy after sleeping on his office couch. He refused to go home until his team was out of danger. "Wolf here," he croaked—his throat dry and eyes bloodshot.

"Wolf, this is Jimmy. We're fifty miles south of last night's location and have taken the east fork. We're still on a float. Lost one package, I repeat, we lost Rag Three. Rag One still here for unwrapping at home. We will need help with that special delivery. Do we have a mailbox location yet?"

"Negative at this time, Jimmy. Cross the big border where mailboxes are easier to come by. When you are over the line, call back and we will find a location, out."

Chris hung up and disassembled the phone with Julia, then packed it in his watertight bag. He turned back to his men.

"Okay, listen up. Best I can make out with my little toy here, we have the Argentinean border on our right and the Brazilian border on our left. A pickup in Paraguay was impossible, but once we get back into Brazil, life is a little easier. I like the water as much as the next guy, but I'm getting tired of being wet. I'll track our position and we'll exit to the left bank which should be Brazil. Then we'll move overland and try and arrange an exit. Some bad news, I'm afraid. We moved a lot further last night than I planned. We way overshot Raul. I'm afraid Santos stays where he is. I'm sorry fellas. I've never left anyone behind. There's nothing I can do about that now. We're forty miles downstream now. I'll see his parents myself when we get home. This is on me, not you guys. I'm sorry."

He turned around and faced forward, feeling like crap. Julia leaned closer and whispered in his ear. "Hey, I know you didn't want to leave him behind. The guys know it, too. But you saved every one of us with this crazy raft of yours. If we had gotten off the river to try and find his body, we'd all probably be dead by now."

He patted her hand, which was around his waist again. "Thanks. I know it was the right decision. But it sucks anyway. Leaving his body to rot in the jungle…shit. His parents don't even have anything to bury. I always said I'd never leave a man behind."

"Chris, he was dead. You saved the living. Now get us the hell out of here so we can all get home alive."

He nodded his head and grunted, and took out the GPS computer again, zooming in on their location as he tried to find the closest landmark in Brazil. He leaned back over his shoulder and nudged Julia.

"Hey tour guide, you ever hear of a town called Salgado Filho?"

"I've never been there, and don't know anything about it other than the fact that it has a small airport. We tried bringing supplies in from there once, but the roads were a mess through the highlands. Even though it's much closer than Santos, the travel time was doubled, and that was assuming a truck would even make it through the crazy mountain roads. We're talking single lanes, no guard rails, mudslides—you getting the picture?"

"Yeah, I think so. But it has an airport. That's all I care about right now. I think you and Theresa may be going back to your school the long way."

"Like, how long's the long way?"

"Like, through Virginia," said Cascaes.

"I can't do that, Chris. I've already been gone for a few days without any word. My Guaranis are going to be worried, and people will start nosing around my office in town if no one can get in touch with me. If I don't get back soon, it could compromise my cover."

"Julia, I read you loud and clear, but right now, this mission has priority until my boss tells me otherwise. I will advise him of your concerns."

"Yeah? Well I have a boss to answer to as well, and maybe you'd better speak to her before you go and screw up a few years of my work down here," she snapped back.

He turned around and looked her in the eyes. "I am not here to screw up your mission. But I have lost a man trying to get this package home, and right now, that is the chief objective. We are getting off of this river and figuring out what happens next. Until then, just relax and wait and see what happens. We are all still a very long way from home, okay?"

"Fine," she said coolly.

Cascaes called back to his men to start working towards the left bank. The river was quiet and free of other boats in the wee morning hours. It was tough maneuvering a mess of trees that was supposed to be a boat, and eventually Moose and Ripper said screw it and hopped in the water, holding one side of the trees and kicking their feet to push towards the shore. McCoy and Cohen had the others help secure their packs, then slid into the water also to help start kicking. Cascaes and O'Conner, in the rear, kept a sharp lookout for anything in the water that might pose a threat. Theresa couldn't even look at them, picturing Moose being eaten by piranhas.

It took ten minutes of hard swimming to get the raft close enough to the bank for it to snag in the soft muddy bottom. Cascaes slid off the front and pulled the bow of the makeshift raft as far as he could, with the other four pushing from the other side.

"Okay people, let's move quickly and quietly, and get into cover as fast as we can. Jones, the prisoner is yours. You are free to filet him if you gives you any trouble—you hear that, Raman? Behave yourself—I'm just waiting for an excuse to feed your ass to the fish," barked Cascaes. He helped Julia down off the raft, not because she needed his help, but because he wanted to. She slid down the mess that was their boat into his arms, and they were face to face for a second. She was still pissed at him, but couldn't help wanting to hug him. She thanked him curtly instead and pulled her pack down over her shoulder.

The team finished unloading people and cargo, then Moose and Ripper cut apart the ropes and netting and pushed the trees apart to float away inconspicuously. The team moved quickly away from the water into the woods, which were more forest than jungle. Cascaes sent Woods and Koches ahead to find a spot where they could dry out for a while and rest. They returned in fifteen minutes with big smiles.

"We have our new home away from home, skipper," said Koches cheerfully, trying to catch his breath.

He led them up a steep, rocky hill. The top was so steep they had to pull themselves hand over hand to get to a small plateau. At the top of this ledge was a small cave in the rocks, and it was dry and fairly open, making it bright inside. Standing atop the ledge, they could see for a hundred miles over the top of the jungle and river below.

"Wow. This was some spot—good job, fellas," said Cascaes. He smiled for the first time in quite a while. All of the men were immediately in a better mood as they took off their boots and muddy wet socks, followed by their cargo pants and shirts. Theresa and Julia, although a bit self-conscious, were too uncomfortable to really care, and followed suit down to their panties and t-shirts. The men broke out some dry towels and gave them to the ladies to use first, averting their gaze as best they could. The women stepped into the shelter of the cave opening to dry off, then threw the towels back out to the men.

Mackey and Woods built a fire, no longer concerned with being chased by Guaranis or terrorists. They were in the mostly uninhabited western border of Brazil, and anyone that would be close enough to smell a campfire, wouldn't give a darn. When the fire was roaring, the men put together some tree limbs and hung their clothes nearby to dry. The two black sport bras hanging near the camouflage pants were a funny contrast as the two women sat closest to the fire wearing bright yellow Los Angeles Ministries t-shirts.

The men prepared MREs and boiled water from the river, then added pills to it to make it safe to drink. They all sat around together like Boy Scouts on a holiday weekend, trying not to stare at the pretty legs across the campfire. Cascaes and Mackey set up the phone and sipped hot coffee, a treat on this sunny but somewhat cooler morning. Their feet were still pruned from being wet for so long, and the sun-warmed rocks that they were standing on felt perfect.

Darren Davis's secure phone rang a world away in his sterile looking office, where he sat across a desk from Dex Murphy and Leah Pereira.

"Wolf here," he said on the second ring.

"Wolf, this is Jimmy. We have crossed the big border and are on our home field again. Rag One is still with us and our team is in shape to play, but we sure would like to get back to our stadium. I just turned on the transponder to show you our exact location. It should be showing up any second. I have the two extra players we picked up in-country, and they are concerned about showing their cards. I request a mailbox, ASAP, and suggest bringing the extra players home, but they are not happy about that. Awaiting instructions, over."

Julia and Theresa sat at the other side of the campfire watching the two of them on the phone and knowing it concerned them, but gave them their privacy knowing it wasn't their decision anyway. Wolf asked Jimmy to sit tight and leave the line open, as the three of them in Langley discussed their course of action. They ended up telling Cascaes to sit tight and wait for a call back in fifteen minutes as they scrambled over to the situation room to locate the team on a real time map.

They reassembled in the room downstairs after they called the director to update him on the mission and tell him they would be back in contact with the team. He was up to his eyeballs in another mission on the other side of the world and left it to Davis and Pereira to work it out. They pulled up the satellite maps and found the transponder signal, then zoomed in on the team.

The map showed the signal coming from a remote area near the Rio Uruguay. It was in the second most southerly state of Brazil, Santa Catarina. Leah looked at their location and zoomed out a bit at their surroundings.

"They aren't that far from Salgado Filho. It's a rough trip on foot, maybe a few days, but there is an airport there. What about a helicopter out of Salgado Filho to pick them up and bring them back to that airport, and then a plane to bring them home?" asked Leah.

"Possible, if we can get a bird down there. What about your two agents? Cascaes said they weren't keen on leaving their location. I think Julia is a bit attached to her people down there," said Davis.

Leah made a scowl. "It's partly my fault. I have encouraged her involvement down there because it assuaged my own guilt for the things I have done over the years and I know it made her feel good as well. But she was down there to work CIA operations, not teach and feed the natives. She just helped pull off the biggest mission of her South American career, and now it's time for her and Theresa to get the hell out of there. I'm shutting it down as of now. I want them home with your men."

Davis exhaled slowly and crossed his arms thoughtfully. "Okay then, that's final. Do you have decent contacts in Brazil that might help with a bird? Maybe we pick them up and just get them to the Atlantic. I can have a sub waiting for them within twenty-four hours. We've had them on standby down there since last week."

Leah clucked her tongue and thought for a moment. "It may cost some money and some future favors, but yeah, I can get us a chopper. It needs to be a large one. We've got twenty passengers? It makes it a little more complicated."

"Yeah. We'll need a large transport helicopter. Got anything like that lying around?"

"Only one comes to mind, and this is going to be very interesting. Better leave that part to me. Tell our people what's up, and give me a couple of hours to arrange for their pickup. Maybe just have them stay where they are for now."

Leah hustled off to her own office, and Darren looked at Dex and shrugged. He called back Cascaes on the satellite phone.

"Jimmy here," said Cascaes anxiously.

"Wolf here with an update. For now, I want you to stay where you are. We are attempting to arrange a FedEx truck to pick up the whole shipment. Sit tight and I will contact you again ASAP. Now I need to speak directly with the teacher."

"Roger that, Wolf, wait one," he said, and then turned towards Julia. "Jules!" he shouted. "Um, you have a phone call."

Julia ran over to him, wearing only the oversized yellow t-shirt which she held down against her thighs. She had nothing on underneath, and Cascaes was having a difficult time not staring at the hard nipples poking out of the thin yellow material. He cleared his throat and looked away as he handed her the phone. She was maybe the best looking woman he'd ever seen in his life, and he still hadn't even seen her with makeup or in normal clothes.

"Teacher, here," she said, expecting to hear Leah's voice. Instead it was Darren Davis.

"Teacher this is Wolf. Jaguar has just left my office. You are instructed, directly by Jaguar, to return with Jimmy and the package. School is closed, Teacher."

Julia felt her stomach drop. "Wolf, I'd like to speak to Jaguar directly."

"Negative, Teacher. School is closed, and that is official. You are to return with Jimmy and that is a direct order. We are making arrangements now. Sit tight and await further instructions. Get Jimmy back on the horn."

Julia felt sick. She handed the phone to Cascaes, fighting back tears. She hadn't even had a chance to say goodbye to any of her people. He took the phone from her, pretty sure of what had been said. "Jimmy here."

"Jimmy, sit tight. I will try and get back to you with a few hours. Turn your transponder off and remain on location. Wolf out."

Cascaes looked at her, but she turned her back and walked off to sit next to the fire with Theresa again. She leaned over and told Theresa that their mission was pulled and the outreach program had ceased to exist. They'd be going home with the team.

Theresa was stunned. "What about the office? Who's going to do the immunizations and get the supplies down there?"

Julia looked at her and started weeping, then hugged her and said "No one! No one, Theresa!" through her tears. "They closed the whole fucking thing! We don't even get to say goodbye."

The other members of the team looked at each other nervously. They felt awkward, not only because the two women were half naked and not paying attention to their t-shirts riding up their exposed legs and behinds, but because they were both crying hard in front of everyone. Moose took off his t-shirt and threw it over their exposed legs, then poured them two cups of coffee as the others got up and pretended to be busy adjusting their clothes over the fire. They added wood and kicked up the flames. Moose knelt down and gave them each coffee. They thanked him as they wiped off their faces with the backs of their hands.

They sipped the hot coffee and gave smiles to Moose, who patted their shoulders and gave them some privacy. Julia took a deep breath. "I'm so pissed, Theresa. *Years* of my life down there just taken away without even a conversation about it. *Nothing!* I should just quit and go back on my own."

Theresa frowned. "Julia, the program worked because the CIA funded it. If they close it down, it's closed. We have no other resources. Whatever good we did, it's done. We helped a lot of people the last few years. It was never why we were there—don't forget that."

"I know it wasn't why we were there, but we did more for those people in three years than their own government did in three hundred. They aren't going to understand why we just *left*. All they are going to know is that we abandoned them without so much as a fucking goodbye." She was crying again.

"Get a hold of yourself. Julia, we work for CIA. We had a great cover and did a lot of good, on our own, beyond the job description. But don't forget what Vega and those other animals did to the locals. He's out of business now, thanks partly to us, and the butchers who killed McKnight and all of his staff are either dead or going to Langley," she said, pointing to the cuffed and blindfolded Raman, who sat next to Jones.

"I am upset to be leaving without a chance to say goodbye, too, Julia. But when I left Fallujah I didn't get to say goodbye to all my marine friends, either. And some of them never made it home. Don't forget why we work for CIA, Julia. We help as many people with our real work as we did with the cover story. Remember *that*."

Theresa sipped her coffee and let her words sink in. Julia stopped crying and sipped her coffee, too, then patted Theresa's arm. "Okay," she said quietly, "Just need to make some mental adjustments, ya' know?"

As soon as the clothes were dry, everyone redressed. McCoy combined a bunch of MREs into some kind of buffet concoction which seemed better than the meals individually, and they all ate together, quietly enjoying the view of the green landscape below, divided by the meandering brown river.

Cascaes sat down next to Julia, their feet hanging over the edge of the ledge.

"Some view, huh? How ya' feelin'?" he asked quietly

"Okay, I guess."

He sat playing with his food for a while. "I'm sorry about all this. I know those people meant a lot to you."

Julia looked at him, no longer mad at him, but frustrated at the whole situation. "It's just that we had *just* gotten the school built, ya' know? The kids were so excited. Things were really improving down there, and I had so many connections. I could have worked this deal another ten years," she said.

"Yeah, I guess so. I know the kids will miss you. I kind of miss them myself, even if it was only a couple of days. You see how they took to Moose? That was too funny."

"Yeah," she said with a smile. She looked at the big man, engaged in conversation with Theresa. "He's probably the biggest human being they've ever seen."

Cascaes smiled and saw him smiling and laughing with Theresa. "Yeah, his heart's that big, too. I mean, he's as tough as they get, and I'll go to war with him anytime, but he's really a big teddy bear. I think he likes Theresa."

"No shit," she said with a laugh. "And Theresa is tough as nails on the outside, too, but she's also a sweetheart. And fearless."

"Sounds like you," said Chris.

"I don't know. I don't scare easily—and I've done my share of crazy missions, but I don't hide my emotions as well as she does."

"So if I can't read anything, it's because nothing is there?" he asked.

She smiled and cocked her head at him. "Ya' know, I was really pissed at you before. Kinda' held you responsible for my being pulled out of here. But really, I know it isn't on you, the company was going to do whatever they were going to do regardless of my opinion. That being said, what happens if we both end up back in Virginia?"

"What do you mean," he asked cautiously.

"I mean, are you still taking me on a real date? So far, your idea of dinner and a night out isn't all that great."

"I'd love to take you out when we get back. No fooling." He said with a smile.

"Good," she said. "Because as Theresa says, I kinda' *like* you, like you."

Cascaes was dying to kiss her, but eighteen other people behind him prevented him. She read his mind. "Try in Virginia, and I'll let you," she said.

He laughed out loud. "Deal!"

Their private conversation was interrupted by the beep of his satellite phone. It was back by Mackey, who grabbed it.

"Jimmy Two here, over."

He was surprised to hear Leah's voice instead of Davis's.

"This is Jaguar," she said in her lightly accented voice. "FedEx is coming, but not in a standard truck. Do not be alarmed at the delivery truck. It was the only one I had that is the proper size. I repeat, do not be alarmed. Time to your location, two hours from now. It will bring you to a wet location for a silent return. Understand?"

Mackey was trying to catch up, but Cascaes had been listening as soon as he ran over. "Silent pickup—a sub, Mac," he whispered.

Mac nodded. "Okay Jaguar. Inbound Fedex in two hours, to a wet drop and silent trip back. Roger that. Over."

"See you in a couple of days, Jimmy Two. Safe trip. Over and out."

Cascaes smiled and patted Mackey on the shoulder. "Okay people, listen up. We have two hours to enjoy the scenery and then an inbound chopper is taking us out of here. I have no idea what to expect, but I take it from what was said that the helicopter isn't a standard ride. We need a large helo, so she grabbed what she could. She said not to be alarmed, so stay cool. We are being taken to the Atlantic for a submarine pickup and return to Langley. Police up this area and make sure we leave nothing behind. Any questions?"

Hodges mumbled something about "not signing up for any submarine ride", but no else said anything. They all settled back down and enjoyed the sunshine.

Mackey walked over to Ripper. "Ripper, you take watch on Qasim. We're getting close to take-off time and he may get spooked. You're bigger than Earl, so you take watch on him now. He moves, you sit on him. We've come too far to lose him now. I want the boys in Langley to pump this piece of shit for information for the next ten years."

Cascaes walked back over to the ledge and sat next to Julia. "So what's your real name?" he asked.

"What's yours?" she countered.

"Chris, just like it says on my enlistment papers."

She laughed. "Until I am told otherwise, it's Julia. Besides, it adds to the mystery."

"Great. I'll probably never be able to find you when we get back."

"Oh, don't worry,' she said. "I'm a spy. *I'll* find *you!*"

They sat and enjoyed the view for a while longer, their pinkies touching, which was as close as they could get to holding hands with the team behind them. After a while, Chris stood up and pulled her up with him, and they rejoined the rest of the team. Ryan O'Connor, the SEAL's closest thing to a medic, leaned over to Cascaes. He was a religious guy, and asked his skipper if they could say a prayer for Raul before they left the jungle. Cascaes felt a hammer in his heart when Ryan asked him, and he just nodded his head, yes.

O'Conner called everyone together, except Ripper, who stood up behind the seated prisoner, and they got into a large circle. Julia wasn't really sure what they were doing, but she was happy to have an excuse to hold Chris's hand.

"Before we leave this place, I want to take a minute to say goodbye to our friend Raul Santos. He was a great marine, a great American, and a great friend, and we'll miss him very much. Our Father, who art in Heaven…"

The rest of them prayed with Ryan, then took a moment of silence. Jones and Hodges, who had known Raul the longest, gave each other a big hug and a few smacks on the back. Hodges, imitating Santos, said, "Suck it up—ooraa," quietly to Jones, who smacked his arm and returned the "ooraa."

An hour later, the sound of rotor blades thumping over the jungle brought the men to their feet. Hodges pulled out his powerful binoculars and handed them to Mackey, who looked for a long time before he handed them to Cascaes and said, "You gotta' be shittin' me."

"What is it?" asked Cascaes as he took the binoculars.

"I think it's Marine One," said Mackey incredulously.

Cascaes looked in the distance at the inbound helicopter. It did look a lot like the President of the United State's personal helicopter. The colors looked right and there was some kind of big seal on the door.

"No way," was all Cascaes could muster. He kept watching through the binoculars as the chopper got closer. After a few minutes passed and he could see better, he smiled. "No, Mac. It's way too big. Looks like a Chinook, which makes sense. Not too many choppers can hold this many people."

"It looks like Marine One," said Mackey.

"I think it's the Brazilian version. It does look a lot like one of ours. Some type of official seal on the door, but it's not American." He started laughing. "She wasn't kidding when she said we'd be surprised." He turned to the team. "Okay people, looks like our ride is on the way in. If we move back towards the cave, there should be enough room for it to set down right here."

The men moved back towards the cave and Ripper held tight to their prisoner. They all watched in silence as the large blue and white twin rotor aircraft made a bee-line for them. Cascaes waved a yellow shirt at them and finally moved back with the others. The closer it got, the more they could appreciate the size of the helicopter. It was a very formal looking aircraft, with some type of presidential-looking seal on the doors, and a Brazilian flag on the front.

Julia walked over to Chris. "Jesus Christ—do you know whose helicopter that is?"

"Not a clue, ma'am. But if you'd like to tell us, we'd sure appreciate it," said Cascaes.

"That's the Vice-President of Brazil's personal helicopter. I have met that man on more than one occasion. We all better pray that he isn't on board, or I may be in serious trouble."

"Oh great," said Cascaes as he watched it get closer. "Theresa! Quick! Get me some bandages! A bunch!"

Theresa didn't ask questions, she just ripped open her field pack and pulled out some pressure bandages and gauze and ran to Cascaes. "What's up, Senior Chief?" She asked.

"Cover up this pretty face ASAP," he said pointing to Julia. "We don't want her recognized. Just Bandage her up and we'll say she was injured. You don't let anyone take it off of her until we get out of here. Just make sure she can see. Julia, if you see anyone you recognize, ask for pain medicine and we'll make it look like you are sleeping so nobody bothers you. Hustle up, Theresa."

By the time the chopper circled the small landing area, Julia was bandaged pretty well around her head and face, and no one would recognize her. The chopper slowly descended, blowing dirt and leaves everywhere, and the massive four wheels touched down at the very edge of the plateau. The pilot was signaling to hurry, as he was barely touching the ground, and a flight crewman opened the side door and let the ramp fall out. Mackey ran ahead first, trying to size up who was rescuing them.

"Request permission to come aboard, sir!" he said, sounding very formal.

A Brazilian crewman was pulled out of the way by a man in a business suit who stuck his face close to Mackey. "This helicopter belongs to Vice President Jose Manuel Jerez, and we are under orders to bring you to an off-shore location. Get your people on board and have them sit in the rear of this aircraft. You were never here and I never met you, now move it."

The man was obviously not very happy to be here, but they *did* have a helicopter, and Mackey wasn't concerned about the service or on-board movie or meal. He turned around and yelled for everyone to move, and the team hustled into the helicopter. Cascaes pretended to help Julia aboard and took her to the rear of the aircraft as far away from any strangers as possible. As soon as they were on board, the pilot had them off the ground and headed due east, flying over the jungle at a hundred and fifty miles per hour. The man in the suit walked back only once to the main cabin, which was first class all the way, and stood there with his hands on hips looking disgusted. He shook his head, cursed in Portuguese, and walked back to the cockpit area, closing the door behind him.

Julia whispered to Cascaes, "That's Vice President Jerez'
chief of staff. I have no idea what kind of favors got called in
for this, but you can be sure somebody's ass was in the hot-
seat for this."

"Does he know you?" asked Cascaes.

"No, I just recognize his face. I better stay under wraps until
we get out of here though, I don't know who else is up there."

"Okay," said Cascaes, then he leaned over and whispered,
"But I miss seeing your face." He couldn't see her smiling
under the bandages.

Cascaes and Mackey typed out a message on his little
computer and hit send, telling Langley that they were aboard
the VP's helicopter headed east. The two of them sat back and
relaxed slightly for the first time in quite a while, enjoying
the comfort of the padded leather seats. The inside of the
helicopter was leather and mahogany, and was nicer than any
aircraft any of them had ever been on. The men sat in silence,
each lost in his own thoughts as they headed towards the
waiting submarine.

CHAPTER 40

The passengers, exhausted and hungry, had settled into a semi-sleep. Ripper and Moose sat on each side of the prisoner, who had in fact fallen asleep. After a few hours, the same angry man in the suit reappeared, no cheerier than the last time.

He announced to everyone and no one that they would be arriving as requested in the middle of nowhere. Since there was no place to land, he assumed that they would be going for a swim. And with that, he disappeared again.

Cascaes leaned over to Julia. "You can swim, right?"

She pulled down the bandage to see his face better. "You're kidding, right?"

"Well?"

"Yes, I can swim, but I've never jumped out of a helicopter before!"

"Yeah, well hopefully, today won't be the day to start. The sub should be out here waiting. If this pilot is any good, he'll get us right over it and you'll simply hop down to the deck. The crew down there will get you inside. I suggest you take off the bandages now in case you end up in the water." He stood up and moved forward.

"Okay people, we should be on station in a few minutes. Right before we go, Ripper, you free his hands. We'll hop down, get in, and get the hell out of here. Everyone buddy up in case anyone goes in the drink. They'll have rescue swimmers waiting for us, but I want everyone having a buddy anyway.

Your buddy goes in the drink, you go after him. Moose, you've got Theresa. Julia, you're with me."

The men made a few quiet comments about the skipper getting the babe, but they geared up and assembled by the exit door. Five minutes later, Mr. Pissed-Off Suit Man reappeared. "Apparently, a very large submarine decided to appear here in the middle of nowhere. We will get you down as close as possible. Let me repeat that you were never on this aircraft and we never saw you people. We'll close the door behind you." Apparently, by the look on his face, not fast enough.

The men looked out the portholes at a huge nuclear submarine lying in the water like a giant black whale. It was an Ohio-Class submarine, 560 feet long. Hatches were opening and sailors were running around very busy on the exposed deck. The chopper stopped moving forward and slowly descended until it was almost touching the deck at the far stern end of the sub, away from the con tower. The sub was dead in the water, and its exposed deck was almost twenty feet above the waterline. A crewman from the helicopter opened the door and stepped away, obviously as thrilled to be here as the man in the suit.

One at a time, following Mackey, the team and its prisoner jumped down to the massive submarine. Submariners were quick to grab their guests and lead them to hatchways where they could get inside before anyone ended up swimming. The Captain of the ship was standing on top of the bridge, looking down at his rescue operation. The helicopter circled up and away and disappeared back towards Brazil as the team descended into the sub one at a time for a long trip home.

As the team made their way through the cramped corridors, the submariners stepped out of their way and allowed them to pass. They followed an ensign down the skinny hall, down two flights of stairs, and into a very cramped crew quarters area, where they were told they would have use of the ten bunk beds that were there. The Ensign looked at the two women and said,

"My apologies, ma'ams, we weren't expecting any women. I'll have to see if I can find any room in the ladies quarters."

Theresa laughed at him. "Listen, bud, we've been living with these smelly animals for a few weeks already. Another couple of days won't kill us. We're fine here."

"Yes, ma'am," said the ensign. "It is against navy regs though, ma'am, and I'll have to clear it with the captain."

A voice filled the room from behind them, causing the ensign to snap to attention and bark, "attention on deck." It was the captain, a tall man of about fifty with a white crew cut and matching beard, something submariners were famous for when at sea. "As you were, ensign. These people aren't *on* this boat, son, and because they don't exist, they aren't subject to our regulations. Now which of you ghosts is in charge of your merry band?"

Mackey stepped forward. "That would be me, captain. And this here is Senior Chief Ghost Number Two," he said with a smile and a handshake.

The captain shook hands and asked the two men to follow him, instructing the others to relax for ten minutes, and then he'd get them fed.

Cascaes and Mackey followed the captain down the cramped hallway to his wardroom. They sat at a small table and he poured them each a cup of excellent coffee. It was so good they wanted to cry. Cascaes took a sip and immediately asked if he could get some coffee to his people, and was told not to worry, the captain had a special treat for them. After two minutes of small talk, the captain shifted to serious talk.

"Gentlemen, this ain't my first rodeo. I have taken Special Ops teams in and out of places more times than I can remember. But I have to tell you, this is the first time I've seen such a large team appear on my radar at the last minute like this. You were an unscheduled stop, to say the least. I trust your mission was successful?"

Mackey cleared his throat. "Captain, we very much appreciate your picking us up. More of a rescue really. I'm not sure any of us would have made it out if not for you and your boat. May I ask what you were told, sir?"

The captain laughed. "As usual, I wasn't told jack-shit. I was given an emergency message for a special ops pickup and this location and time. I was expecting a helicopter, but not quite the kind that showed up."

Cascaes laughed. "We said the same thing, sir."

"Am I wrong, or was that a presidential aircraft?"

"Vice-president, sir, but we weren't on that helicopter any more than we are here on your submarine, if you get my drift," said Mackey with a smile.

"Right. Interesting. But you were satisfied with the results of your mission?"

Mackey and Cascaes looked at each other. Cascaes cleared his throat. "The mission objectives were met, sir, but we lost a good man. Worse yet, I had to leave him behind."

The Captain read his face. "Senior chief, is it?"

"Yes, sir," said Cascaes.

"Well, senior chief, listen up. In my twenty odd years in this man's navy, I have lost more than one sailor. And at sea, when we deliver a sailor to the Almighty via a resting place at the bottom of the deep, I'm not sure it feels any different than sleeping in the earth or in ashes. We aren't always offered the luxury of bringing our people home to rest, son. Losing is man is the worst thing that happens to an officer, but it *happens*. Now you put that to rest for your own sanity and keep on doing your job. That's my whole speech on that subject."

He sat back and sized up the two men in front of them, then told them about their journey home. "We will have a day and half submerged, then link up with the fleet and transfer you to a carrier that will fly you home, wherever that is. Showers are limited aboard this boat, gentlemen, but in your case, we will make an exception. I'll have a bunch of clean clothes dropped off at your crew quarters. One of my men will come get you in an hour and you will be treated to the best mess we can offer. Judging from the look of your people, you haven't had a hot meal in a while."

Mackey smiled. "Mighty nice of you, Captain. And that would be a big affirmative on that."

"Unless you count the caterpillars," said Cascaes quietly.

"I don't even want to know," said the Captain with a smile.

⊕

The Captain wasn't lying. The team took quick showers and put on gray sweat suits that simply said "Navy" across the chest. Cascaes couldn't help but think how cute Julia looked in the sweatshirt and imagined her waking up wearing his old one. After they cleaned up, they were taken to the officer's mess and treated to lobster and steak dinners, complete with one cold beer each. The prisoner had been transferred to the brig, a small cell with one cot, and given a much simpler dinner. They ate in privacy, and enjoyed their first real meal in a few weeks. They clinked bud cans to Santos, and the team toasted their two bosses for getting them home.

As soon as dinner was over, everyone 'hit the headwall'. The adrenaline that had kept them going for the past week was gone, and now after an excellent meal and a beer, they were crashing. The two Chrises announced it was "bedtime," and no one argued. They returned to their small sleeping quarters and dropped into the racks. Theresa and Julia took the two furthest in the back, with Julia in the bottom bunk. When she whispered goodnight to Chris, it was torture, knowing she was only a few feet away in the next bunk. They lay on their sides, facing each other and smiling, but were both fast asleep in minutes. Not one person in the room moved for the next seven hours.

CHAPTER 41

By the time the submarine linked up with the fleet, the team was rested, well-fed and anxious for some fresh air. More than one member of the team had commented on how they'd go crazy living on a sub for more than a couple of days. The day and a half of downtime was good therapy. The team joked, talked, ate well, napped, and generally got to know each other better and heal their minor cuts, bruises, and abrasions. It also gave Moose and Theresa more time to realize they really did like each other. Chris and Julia were already goners.

The team was limited to spending almost all of their time in the small sleeping quarters or in the mess, since space was so limited and they didn't want to be in the way. The Captain had taken Cascaes and Mackey to the bridge and given them a little tour to be polite, but they didn't want to overstay their welcome, and didn't stick around long.

When they arrived at the fleet, they surfaced next to a submarine tender and the Captain used the transfer of personnel as an excuse to get some supplies, including fresh fruit, as well as mail for his crew. Prior to picking up the team, they had been at sea for four months, most of that time submerged. After the sub surfaced, the Captain allowed his men topside in shifts to see the sun and breath some fresh air. Three small boats from the *USS Ronald Reagan* arrived at the sub and the team said their goodbyes and thanks to the Captain and crew. Their "package" was taken in an orange jumpsuit with his wrists shackled to his waist, the word *prisoner* in bold letters across his chest and back.

The three small boats bounced across the choppy Caribbean Sea, the SEAL members of the team beaming with joy at being on top of their ocean again. Most of them actually had their faces turned into the mist to deeply breathe the salt air, like addicts needing a fix. Theresa laughed at Moose as he leaned over the edge of the boat, trying to get his face wet with the ocean spray. The SEALs were just a different breed.

The team went from small rubber boats to one of the fleet's largest ships, where they were taken to the flight deck and a waiting master chief standing by an MV-22 Osprey. The master chief welcomed his guests and informed them that he didn't have a 737 commercial airliner hanging around. The Osprey, a Marine Corps tilt-rotor aircraft that could take off vertically, was one of the few aircraft on board the carrier that could handle so many passengers. The Ospreys were new arrivals for the marines on board and would be getting some work in the Middle East when the fleet made its way back across the Atlantic in another month. For now, the fleet was doing some training and had picked up and dropped off personnel at Gitmo in Cuba.

The team boarded the Osprey and was on their way to Puerto Rico within a few minutes. There, a waiting private jet sat, fueled and ready to go back to its home in Langley, Virginia. As the Osprey touched down in Puerto Rico where they would change planes, Julia leaned over to Chris and smiled. "I'll never complain about an indirect flight again for the rest of my life, I promise."

CHAPTER 42

Home

The first cheer happened when the pilot told his passengers that they were in US airspace. The second occurred when they touched down in Langley. Well, everyone was cheering except their guest in the orange jumpsuit who was still complaining about his handcuffs. He shut up when Moose asked him how he thought Vega's wrists were feeling right about now.

The tired but happy passengers stepped down off the sleek black jet and were met by the familiar bus and the smiling face of Dex Murphy. He shook hands firmly with his old friend Chris Mackey and then greeted each member of the team one at a time with a word or two of praise and thanks and a "welcome home." They boarded the bus and were taken directly to the main building where they would be debriefed. Raman Qasim was handed off to two very stoic looking gentlemen and one woman, intentionally chosen for her gender to further humiliate their Islamic prisoner. He was put into a black SUV and taken elsewhere, not to be seen again by any member of the team.

The team walked back into the familiar building and Dex led them back to the large briefing room where Darren Davis and Leah Pereira were waiting to greet them. Leah shook hands with Julia and Theresa and congratulated them on their success, but Julia was quick to snap back that she'd like a chance to speak with Leah alone. Leah told her that there would be private debriefings later for her and Theresa, but for now to join her teammates in the larger room.

Davis was first up to address the room. His first order of business was to inform the team that there was a gold star being engraved at the CIA's memorial near the entranceway for Raul Santos. Santos' family would be informed that he was killed in action on special assignment, but that unfortunately, his body could not be recovered due to the circumstances of the operation. The room was silent when he finished, and then Cascaes told Davis he would be putting Santos in for a Bronze Star and Purple Heart to which Davis simply answered, "Of course." Although he was on assignment to the CIA, for the sake of his family, he would be treated as a United States Marine, killed in combat in the Global War on Terrorism. He would receive full military honors.

Davis lowered the lights and projected pictures on the screen that Cascaes and Mackey had sent in from the field. Everyone cringed at the grainy picture of Enrique Antonio Vega hanging between the two poles with his guts hanging out. Davis quickly changed the slide. When he had finished showing the team the field ID pictures, he showed the slide of McKnight's convoy and the destruction that had occurred during that attack, and then flicked the lights on.

"James McKnight and over thirty other people died because of Enrique Vega and those other three men. You have ended his operation. His cocaine will no longer show up on our streets and the Islamic Fundamentalists in the area have been dealt a blow. Will others replace them? Of course. But *those four* men will no longer add to the world's problems. This Global War on Terror will continue for many years, and even if it means hunting these animals down all over the globe one or two at a time, we will continue our mission to make sure Americans are safe in their beds."

Davis walked around the small podium and sat on a chair close to the small group. "Look, I don't do politics any more than you do. We are given a mission, and we say, 'yes, sir or yes ma'am,' and we do it to the best of our ability. But I can tell you, the mood around DC is changing. And if Congress decides that our troops are leaving Iraq or Afghanistan before the region is stabilized, it will fall on us to do more than we are already doing. Decisions about nation building or going to war are above our pay grade, but I can predict that we, the CIA, are going to be getting a lot busier in the future.

You men signed on to play a little baseball and do some covert work. It may be time to start practicing your fielding and hitting again. The Los Angeles Outreach Ministry is officially closed. The Navy All-Star Team is not, however."

He looked at Theresa. "And maybe the team needs a trainer to travel with them, as well." Moose used his hand to hide his smile. Davis looked at Julia, "Hell, maybe the team could use a couple of trainers. In any case, the possibilities are there. You will spend the next two days here for debriefings and physicals, and then you'll have a week off to unwind. After that, you'll start playing ball again and wait for the next assignment.

On behalf of Director Holstrum, welcome home and congratulations on completing your mission. We hope that Mr. Qasim will shed some light on the Tri-Border Region that will set them back a couple of years." He called up Leah, who briefly offered her congratulations as well, and then asked Theresa and Julia to follow her when she left. They would spend the next few hours describing in great detail everything that had happened over the past week, as well as a more detailed account of their past year or so living with the Guaranis. Julia threatened to quit on more than one occasion during their heated conversation, but kept coming back to the idea of joining the baseball team with Theresa, and more importantly, Chris.

Theresa and Julia would both be busy for the next few weeks documenting their files from beginning to end of their time in Paraguay. "The good, the bad, and the ugly file" as the agents called them, would be reviewed carefully to try and learn from it for future operations. The contacts in Paraguay would be noted for future operations as well. And while Julia and Theresa were never ultimately satisfied with Leah's decision to close the operation down and pull out, it was over, and in the end, they made their decision to stick it out at CIA.

EPILOGUE

Director Holstrum left St. Peter's Cemetery early that morning after his brief conversation with the white granite stone that read *James McKnight*. He dropped the flowers after he had told his buddy Jim that he got the bastards, and he'd see him again one day down the road.

Chris Cascaes woke up late that same morning. He was face down in fresh smelling soft sheets, and it took him a second to remember where he was. It had been quite a long time since he had slept past eight o'clock in the morning. He lifted his head and turned it the other way to see Julia smiling at him. He grinned and said, good morning. She leaned over and gave him a kiss, and he decided it was going to be another really good day.

In a cell in an undisclosed location, there was no morning or evening. The lights went on and off at random, along with the screaming loud rap music. It had been several very long days indeed for Raman Qasim, who no longer had any idea what day or time it was. He didn't know it, but a very long day was about to start for him.

Moose pulled up in front of Theresa's small apartment. They had enjoyed a couple of dinners together and could see that they would be spending a lot of time together in the future. She hopped in his pickup truck, kissed him good morning, and they took off to grab breakfast before heading over to baseball practice. Moose informed the team trainer, Theresa that he had been cramping up lately and might need a full rub down after

214

practice. She made a face and said, "uh-huh," then punched his big arm. They both laughed, knowing that they were perilously close to pulling back into her driveway.

Dex Murphy's secure phone rang at home. It was his second day off in sixteen days. It was Director Holstrum.

"Sorry Dex, I know you had some time off coming to you. We have a situation in the Democratic Republic of Congo, and I need your team. How long before you can have them ready for another op?"

ABOUT THE AUTHOR

David M. Salkin is the author of thirteen thrillers in various genres, including military espionage, crime, horror, science fiction, action-adventure and mystery. With a writing style reminiscent of the late, great Michael Crichton, Salkin's work keeps his readers turning pages into the late hours. His books have received Gold and Bronze medals in the Stars & Flags book awards, and David has appeared as a guest speaker all over the country.

David is an elected official in Freehold Township, NJ where he has served for twenty years in various roles including Mayor, Deputy Mayor, Township Committeeman and Police Commissioner. He co-owns Salkin's Jewel Case with his brother and is a Master Graduate Gemologist.

When not working or writing, David prefers to be Scuba diving with his family. He is a Master Diver and "fish geek," as well as a pretty good chef and wine aficionado. Some of his famous recipes were perfected in the parking lot of Giants Stadium.